BRIMMING BOUGHS

VANEETA KAUR

Published by Purple Roan Project LTD.
Copyright © 2018
Vaneeta Kaur has asserted her right to be identified as the author of this work.

All rights reserved. No part of this publication may be reproduced, stored or transmitted, in any form or by any means, electronic, mechanical, photocopying, recording or otherwise, without the permission of the author.

This novel is a work of fiction. Names, characters, businesses, organisations, places and events other than those clearly in the public domain, are either the product of the author's imagination or are used fictitiously. Any resemblance to actual persons, living or dead, events or locales is entirely coincidental.

Book cover Design: Clarice Phillips

Illustrations: Harpps Kaur

Editor: Laura McFarlene

Thank you.

The Silver Lining Series has taken me on a beautiful path of self-discovery.

I'm so thankful for the characters that I've created in these novels; they've helped me to question, investigate and recognise the intricate details of the Universe.

However, more so, I'm thankful to those that have supported me in my journey of creating the series. You know who you are. Thank you so much and I love you so dearly.

Blessed be. Peace for all.

Vaneeta x

Feel free to post quotes, paragraphs or your thoughts in relation to Brimming Boughs on your socials tagging #missvaneetakaur so I can like and share.

Brimming Boughs

"Shed all that you were, to bloom into who you were meant to be."

CONTENTS

Part One	1
Part Two	41
Part Three	101
Part Four	136
About the Author	172

Saturday 16th June 1984

Greater London was becoming a diverse and increasingly desirable place to live because of its idyllic homes and cul-de-sacs. Summer was bringing families together in their gardens, either to simply enjoy the outdoors or have barbeques. The air was humid and sticky, and continuous iced water was needed to keep people's mouths from drying. Eighties summer songs roared from the gardens of most of the houses: all except one.

Two young girls were chucking cold water at each other to cool themselves against the heat. Nayla Wood came running down her patterned brown staircase with a towel in her hand, screaming out her daughter's name. Her blonde hair was swinging behind her as she picked up the plate with a sandwich on it from the kitchen on her way outside. Her daughter was too busy enjoying the water being thrown at her to see her mother waiting for her. "Estella!"

Estella sprinted with her dripping hair to her mother, who was now sat on the porch step waiting for her. Nayla wiped her down, then handed over the neatly-cut sandwich.

Estella blinked, "Mummy, where's Robyn's sandwich?" Nayla continued rubbing the tips of Estella's hair, "it's okay Robyn, you can share my sandwich." Estella turned to look at her sister, but was confused to see an empty space next to her. Nayla tutted when her daughter stepped away scanning the small garden. "Robyn?"

Estella continued nibbling at the sides of the sandwich, not stopping to search the garden in hopes of her sister reappearing.

Further down the garden, a young Robyn sat in the corner behind the bushes, digging at the soil harshly with a pitchfork. She stabbed the soil and deepened the hole whilst it slowly became wet with her heavy tears. Her blonde hair stuck to her face along with the flying dirt that hit at her burning red face.

Friday 15th April 1988

"Mum!" Robyn allowed her sister to drag her into the living room by the shoulders before she dropped herself down on the sofa while

Estella screamed up the stairs. "Mum!" Estella came running back to her and dropped herself on the floor in front of her. "What should I do?"

"Don't worry so much Estella. The bleeding will stop." Robyn kept the light smile on her face so that her sister wouldn't worry, even though the slash in her leg boiled beneath her skin.

Estella shook her head, rubbing her sister's knee, "it's my fault. We shouldn't have been running in the rain like that."

Robyn analysed her sister's fluttering eyes. "It's not a big deal." Estella had been the one to suggest racing through the puddles; as the older sister though, Robyn felt like she should've known better. They both had skidded forwards over the puddle. Estella landed safely in the puddle, however, Robyn's leg scraped against the cement, causing a gushing slash right down her leg. "Are you okay though?"

Estella's ponytail bounced up and down with her frantic nodding. "Yeah, yeah!"

They both turned their heads at the pounding noise coming down the stairs, "Estella, what's happened? I heard you screaming."

Robyn dropped her head away from her narrow-faced mother whilst Estella pulled herself up from the floor. "Mum you need to check Robyn's leg! She fell really badly. There was blood everywhere!"

Nayla glimpsed at her daughter, then glanced at Robyn, whose large eyes were avoiding her mother's piercing gaze. Carefully, Robyn lifted her head to meet her mother's sharp features, which made her take in the air around her. Her mother rolled her eyes at her, then looked to Estella. "Sweetie, you're soaking!"

"But Mum–" Estella began in protest.

Nayla bit her lip, "Dry up now, Estella!"

Estella looked at Robyn, who had dropped her head again. Estella huffed before running away and up the stairs, making sure to make her footsteps heard.

Robyn managed to gain the effort to get up from the sofa to aim for the bathroom when Nayla took two large paces towards her, hissing, "try not to get my child involved in your stupid games." Nayla left her shivering with quivering lips.

Monday 25th December 1989

She opened her eyes. Her walls were white and plain. She had a stack of books from the library that she'd never bothered to return. Robyn dug deeper into her blankets, attempting to ignore the scent of freshly cooked spicy mushrooms that reached her room from downstairs.

Her mother and sister had returned yesterday with beaming smiles. Her mother had never warned her that they'd be going away, which left her clueless about where they'd been for the past few days.

After twenty minutes or so, Robyn dragged her heavy body downstairs following the mouth-watering scent. The Christmas tree was sparkling with red and gold tinsel and the ceiling glistened with Christmas lights. Her mother and sister were sitting down at the table, digging into their warm breakfast. They both paid no attention to her entering their bubble of Christmas joy.

"Sweetie, eat up and then you can open your presents." Nayla said to Estella, splitting her sausage in half.

Estella clapped her hands before she scooped beans into her mouth. Robyn was hungry and the smell of the fresh English breakfast was calling her. Her mother watched her remove a plate from the cupboard before sitting down with them at the table. Nayla then swiftly grabbed the plate from beneath her hand, reaching out for the last slice of bread, "darling, do you want this?" Estella's head bobbed up and down.

Robyn took a deep breath, her large brown eyes flickering at her mother who was rolling her eyes at her. The next few minutes filled Robyn's system with despair. Estella and Robyn used to be attached by the hip. They used to do everything together, until their mother built a thick wall between the two of them. Now Estella hardly ever acknowledged her.

"Time for presents Estella!" Robyn watched them both rush to the living room.

Monday 22nd January 1990

Robyn closed the door behind her after experiencing a hard day of heavy words at school. The safety of the four walls of her room screamed to her and the warmth of her bed was what she desired. She had to do what she was about to do though, no matter how horrible the next few minutes were going to be. It had to be done; she couldn't hack any more embarrassment. With her bag still hanging on her shoulder she lugged her worn out feet into the kitchen.

"Mum." Her mother's attention remained on chopping the carrots into thin slices. The absence of Estella rang in the house. Her eyes roamed the kitchen, searching for a bolt of courage that could overtake the chill trickling down her body. She cleared her throat and stroked her thick blonde hair out of her face. "Mum." The knife began hitting the chopping board harder. "Mum, I'm being picked on because of the hole in my shoes. When I went to the teacher, she said that I need new shoes."

The knife came to a halt along with her breathing. Her mother's sharp stare pivoted to her and she felt her brown eyes sear into her. Robyn took a deep breath, holding her trembling body together. "I've had these shoes for quite a while now and I thought as you bought Estella some new clothes last week, it would be okay for you to buy me some new shoes too."

She jumped back, seeing the tip of the knife directed in front of her eyes. Her hands began shaking when mother faced her, "do you really think I want to waste my money on you?"

Water welled in her eyes and she gulped before stepping back. Her chest suddenly felt like it was loaded with fire and rocks.

Friday 15th July 1994

Humidity flooded the science department at Robyn's school. She sat next to a Bunsen burner with her books stacked along the table. Her eyes squeezed in thought, trying to understand the complications of what she was reading.

She was spending the day alone today, otherwise her friend

Tanya and she would be working out the complexity of physics together.

She could hear the children running around outside in the bright skin-tingling heat. She spent most of her lunch hours and free periods in empty rooms, trying to cram all her revision into her mind.

She pulled her hands over her head and tied her long blonde her back to keep it away from her face.

She tried to recite her practice essay back to herself, even though the shouting outside was ringing in her brain. She heard heels tapping against the floorboards behind her and her large brown eyes travelled up from the page, readying herself for whatever verbal abuse was about to come her way.

Estella's extremely high ponytail hung on top of her head in a pink scrunchie. She placed herself on the opposite side of the wooden desk in front of Robyn with her friends on either side and her thick lips formed a smile. The three of them appeared like triplets. Estella and her friends shared the same round faces, high ponytails and banned, bright heels that they managed to get away with.

"Hey Sis. How's it going?" Estella asked squeakily without really wanting an answer.

Robyn began packing her books and tried to refrain from rolling her eyes. She didn't need this, not now. Long fingers slithered onto her essay paper, stopping her from picking it up. She breathed slowly, trying not to show her anxiety. "Could you please remove your hand?"

Robyn directed her face at her sister's friend, Aabha. Her green eyes were sharp when she released a giggle, "No, I want to read this." Robyn's eyes moved to the window, "I didn't know you took psychology Robyn. Did you take it to understand why you're such a loner?"

Estella laughed, "she isn't that much of a loner, she has that weird friend of hers, Tanya. The one that always comes in wearing that ugly lollypop jacket. We need to find a way to burn that."

Robyn ground her teeth, refraining from spitting a nasty remark at her sister. "Give me back my essay please." She attempted to retrieve the paper back, however, Estella's other friend Pari snatched it from Aabha with her long, thin fingers.

Pari's lips curled on her thin face, "with pleasure." Pari tore the paper in half and Robyn shouted, thinking of all the work that had gone into that paper, which was marked by her psychology teacher. She needed those comments. Robyn listened to her sister laughing whilst packing her belongings into her bag. Her mind ignored the sound of the paper being torn in order to focus on leaving the room. Aabha then grabbed her bag and it tipped upside down: all her work fell downwards. Estella and Pari began kicking her books and papers across the floor. Robyn could feel her eyes burning with tears whilst staring at her sister. She ran out of the classroom, hearing the girls laughing behind her.

The heat stuck to her skin. She was sitting at the back of the school field behind all the bushes. No one knew about this place. Not even Tanya. Just her.

The sound of her heartbeat overtook her eardrums. Her chest closed into a ball and her throat hurt from her harsh intake of breath, which never seemed to fill her lungs. Her hands were shaking, and her mind spun in circles trying to comprehend if she felt hot or cold. She closed her eyes as two sledgehammers knocked against the sides of her temple.

There was a small piece of chipped branch next to her. She needed to release her anger. Her hands trembled, picking it up. She inhaled, scraping the piece against her already scarred skin.

Tuesday 19th July 1994

She kept repeating to herself that her exam had gone fine. Her main aim currently was to go to university. She needed to pass all her exams for this to happen. The thought of not having a way out of the house she was living in filled her insides with dark, black dread.

Whilst her sister and mother went bowling, Robyn was invited to stay around Tanya's house; she reluctantly accepted the invite.

Tanya's house was small. It had plain, white painted walls. Of all the rooms in the house, Tanya's was the brightest. She had green wallpaper that made Robyn feel like she had stepped into a wild forest. Robyn sat on Tanya's bed staring at the television. She knew that they were watching a video. It was a romantic film. She remembered having that conversation. However, she couldn't keep up with what it was they were watching or what was happening.

She got up from the bed quietly. She wasn't interested in the film. All romantic movies ended the same way anyway, she thought. The guy chases after the girl to the airport after he realises they are meant to be together and then they live happily ever after. Nothing like reality.

"Where you going?" Tanya asked, wearing her fairy patterned pyjamas. Robyn blinked and pointed at the toilet. "Be quick. I think Edward's going to go back for Vivian." Robyn gave Tanya a thumbs up before walking to the bathroom and locking the door behind her. She took a deep breath, placing her back against the door to slide down onto the marble floor. The coldness of her tears dried against the heat of her skin. Her long, sharp nails scratched her left arm to help her feel the satisfaction of the blood leaking from her skin. The relief paced her breathing.

Saturday 19th February 1994

It was late and the air was bitter. She had no clue where they were. She just jumped in the back of the car with her friends. They brought her to an open field with a big screen. She wished she hadn't joined her crazy friends.

Adara's parents had warned her about going out to late showings. "Don't spend late nights in the cinema, you don't know what happens there," or her favourite, "if you're going to be out late, spend it around one of your friend's houses, at least we can we know you're not roaming the streets at heavens knows what times."

She regretted not listening.

It was an open-air cinema. The kind where they place the big screen in a park and show an old movie. There were about a hundred people there, sitting on the grass on their colourful deckchairs. *Why would anyone in their right mind be interested in attending an open cinema in such a chilling weather?* She thought. It made no sense to her. They were watching a romantic animation. Her friends pestered her to join them, even though she wasn't a fan of animated films. She wanted more popcorn. The rest of the food was in the car. She took a slow walk right to the back of the car park, until she reached her friend's car. She tried to open the boot. It was stuck. She knew she should've sent her friend to get it instead. Whenever she tried to yank it open; it was always stuck. She stopped fighting with the car and then stood for a second to debate on whether to turn back or try again.

The moment she made the decision to turn back, she felt a soft palm go over her mouth. Her eyes flared open. Next thing she knew, something hard ruthlessly made contact with the back of her head, and then everything went black.

TUESDAY 27TH DECEMBER 2011

Kristopher Dauni grumbled at hearing his blackberry ring. His hand snaked out from under the blanket to look at the caller ID. He rolled his eyes, then dragged himself out of bed to sluggishly step down the stairs.

The staircase ran down to the base of the Kensington house that his mother had dotingly designed. The crystal chandeliers shone against the gold marble floor, which extended to a family room, a large dining area, a small living room and a large kitchen. Most of his memories resided in the long, rustic garden where he used to play with his cousin Timothy, who had recently relocated back to London. Though the garden was aesthetically charming and contained many winding pathways, Kris hardly ever went there now.

Luckily, the heated marble floor quickly warmed his body up so that when he opened the door the wintry December air didn't hit him as hard as it would normally for a person during this shivering season. He rubbed his hand through his neat, jet-black hair before he picked up his jingling keys from the side table, wondering if he should have a duplicate made.

"Flipping hell Kris!" Lauren sprang through the door. "Do you realise how long I've been standing out there?" She stormed into the kitchen behind Kris.

Lauren's hair, which she always kept in a ponytail, had grown to shoulder length. Though Lauren still lived in her small, cosy Hammersmith flat, she still seemed to always be on his doorstep in the early hours of the morning, just to bother him about one matter or another. Kris handed her a cup of coffee and tried to escape the kitchen before she could begin. Though Kris wasn't the tallest of men, he was a lot taller than Lauren. He wondered how she had gained the strength to pull him back so swiftly by his arm and direct him in front of her already open laptop. Kris rubbed his head, watching Lauren place her mobile on the counter behind her laptop.

"Right, let's not waste any more of your time, oldie." He rolled his eyes. Lauren tapped enter on the keyboard then the screen showed him a round-faced woman with long blonde hair, and sea-blue eyes.

Kris immediately slammed the laptop shut. She looked at him with her mouth open, ready to shout. "You're becoming annoying. Showing me these endless numbers of women like I'm some kind of..."

"Sad and lonely old man."

Kris's exhaled. "I'm not sad, I'm not lonely and I'm sure as hell not old!"

"Okay fair enough, you're not exactly an old man, but Kris, you're lonely." She put the laptop away and walked up to him, "so you're going to meet this woman. She's one of my high school friends, so I know she isn't a looney. Her name is June and..."

Kris picked up his coffee and let the heat calm his annoyance away. "June. Why not May?"

"Ha ha Kris! You're so funny!" Lauren said rolling her eyes, "I will send you the address, be there on time."

Kris heard the front door slam, telling him that she had left the house. For months, Lauren had been setting him up with other women that she somehow was already friends with. How she knew all these women was beyond his knowledge. He appreciated that she was trying to help him, but he had had enough. She didn't seem to understand that he wasn't interested.

He heard a buzz and immediately his eyes landed on Lauren's mobile on the kitchen counter. His eyebrows lifted in confusion, staring at the caller ID, and he muted it.

Kris sat in his office beating at his keyboard, trying to quickly get down all his thoughts on the screen before they left him. He heard a light knock and Ayva walked in. In addition to the glass window behind him that showed the glorious beauty of Kensington's ancient buildings, the doors to his office were now also glass. He usually left his office door open, unless he was in a meeting. It made him seem more approachable, even though today he didn't feel that way.

Ayva was a tall, brown-eyed, rectangular-faced, quirky woman that had taken some time adjusting to the ways of the office. He finished hitting his keyboard then looked up at her. "I thought I would remind you that you've got Mrs Kallahan in an hour." Kris face dropped straight into his hands. Kallahan was one of the harshest clients he had ever come across. "Do you want me to cancel?" Kris lifted his head, thinking that Lauren had taught her well. He tilted his head side to side; if he didn't get this overdone with now, he'd just keep pushing it back.

In the past few years, Kris had taken a large step back from the control he had in his business. The Dauni's department store and its subsidiaries based in Kensington, were completely managed by Henri and Kris hardly got involved with it. Separate directors managed the restaurant chains, international department stores and Sani's charities. After Kelci had left, he had no interest in branching out further for Dauni's. The conglomerates were running smoothly, and he saw no reason to interfere with it. Kris now only managed the real estate branches in London, whilst his partners took care of the ones outside of London.

After Ayvya walked out, Lauren came strolling in with her ponytail swinging from side to side. Kris removed her phone from his drawer and threw it on the desk. She picked up her mobile and stroked it like it was a guinea pig.

Kris leaned back into his chair to observe Lauren's expression. "You may want to check your missed calls."

Lauren waved her hand. "So, I've texted you the address," she said. Kris tilted his head slightly before turning back to his screen. "Her name is June Avery and you're going to meet her at a Chinese restaur..." Lauren came around the desk and bent down, trying to meet his eyes. "Kris!"

Kris avoided her by focusing on the figures on his screen, "you have work to do. Go."

He saw Lauren straighten up and drop her hands. "I'm only trying to help, you know."

∼

Kallahan's husband had passed away two years ago, leaving her a building with much rich history; like many other buildings in the area. Kallahan wanted to sell and Kris was willing to buy; if the price was right. Kallahan wanted to leave the UK with no strings attached and she wanted money to live off of indefinitely. She knew the price could only rise for this building, nonetheless, for the present moment she was pricing unreasonably. Kris had a lot of money to waste, however he wanted it wasted on the right things. Not a building that he could lose profits on. The first time Kris had spoken to her, he knew she wasn't going to be an easy person to negotiate with. She had no intention of dropping her price and Kris wondered whether his time was being wasted. He was thinking of a way to close this meeting on a positive note without creating any friction.

Ayva knocked and he waved for her to come in. "Kris, I'm sorry, you're late for your eleven o'clock. She's waiting." Kris's owl eyes lingered on Ayva and she smiled like she'd been caught stealing a bottle of alcohol in a shop.

Kallahan's long, black, tight plait swung when she picked herself up from her chair, "I didn't even realise the time. Either way, it was still good to meet you Mr Dauni."

Kris got up to shake her hand. "Kris is fine."

She placed her hands back in her pockets and stepped back. "And, it's just Gal and it was still great to meet you. If you ever decide to change your mind, please let me know."

Kris waited a few seconds and then called Ayva back in. She came into the office in a way that made him feel like a primary school teacher. Ayva stroked her jet-black hair and shifted her legs from one to the other. "Lauren told me that when you keep glancing out the glass door it means you want to leave your office. And your meeting had run over, I assumed that..." Kris's lips turned into a light smile. "Did I do wrong?" He laughed shaking his head. "Did I mess up the meeting?"

Kris put his hand up. "Honestly, no, it was fine. You assumed right. Thank you Ayva. But, I think next time, ring just in case." Ayva nodded before leaving the room. Kris glanced at the clock. He had forty minutes.

The spicy scent of the oriental food hit his senses upon entering the beautifully constructed Chinese restaurant based in Paddington. A tall woman with shoulder-length blonde hair and brown eyes approached him. Her wavy hair seemed effortlessly tied up in a high ponytail that emphasised the doll like roundness of her face. Her shoulders were firmly high, along with her chin, which gave her an air of confidence as she led them to a table that was centred in the middle of the room. "My name is Estella Wood and I'll be serving you. Would you like a drink?"

Kris noticed Estella's large eyes and her soft features. "I'm just waiting for someone."

She placed two menus on the table and nodded. "I'll be back then."

Kris stroked his hair then sighed whilst he took out his blackberry and began searching through some of his unanswered emails. "Are you another phone addict?" Before he could take his eyes off his phone, a small woman sat in front of him whom he recognised straight away: "June Avery."

"Kris Dauni." He held his phone up, "I was just passing time." She made herself comfortable in the chair and immediately threw herself into a lecture about the restaurant; Kris struggled to keep up with her chatter. He shook his head, realising that he couldn't be bothered to talk; he did so anyway to break the awkwardness. "Lauren said she knew you from high school."

June bopped her head up and down, "yeah she used to help me in my maths," she leaned into the table, "help me – by that I mean she would do the work for me." Slow, stringed instrumental music suddenly began playing in background and he wanted it to stop. June giggled to herself whilst he tapped his fingers on his phone, "she said she works for you."

Kris was about to respond when Estella approached them, making June bop her head from side to side. Estella walked away with June's coke order; he exhaled, tapping his blackberry again. "So, what did Lauren say to you to drag you here?" Kris's eyebrows pulled together, and June placed her menu down. "There's no other way to say this so I'll just say it; you don't want to be here." He shook his head, instantly knowing his cheeks were burning. June grinned. "Don't lie."

Kris rubbed the base of his neck, "I'm so sorry. You seem really nice but..." June's eyes whizzed around the restaurant and he felt the blood rush to his cheeks again. "Honestly. I'm a complete..." Kris squeezed his eyelids. "I'm just sorry."

June laughed. "It's okay. You've nothing to be sorry for. I know Lauren can be pushy sometimes. You can go if you like, I can get a friend to meet me."

Kris got up and placed forty pounds on the table, saying apologetically, "well enjoy, the food; my treat." He raised his hand to stop her from resisting. "I'm sorry again. Bye." Kris walked away from the table grinding his teeth. He had never felt so rude in his life.

THURSDAY 11TH AUGUST 1994

It was hot. The heat grazed her skin. The easiest way to keep hold of your possessions was to wear them. The problem was that the overwhelming heat didn't allow her to do that. Eighteen-year-old Robyn placed her bag filled with her clothes at the end of the bench and wrapped her blue jumper into a pillow. Though the sweat was slithering down her skin, she still wrapped her arms around her in fear of feeling exposed. Even though she persistently kept her eyes closed, planks of the bench dug into her skin. The shouting coming from somewhere was keeping her body in alert mode, so instead she stared up at the darkness, not knowing what time it was. The diamond lit sky told her it was late night and the heat told her it was summer. An hour or so passed and sleep struck her eyes.

Something was poking her shoulder. Her eyelids lifted, catching a glimpse of a bearded face before the weight of her eyelids dropped again. A few seconds later, the poking came more harshly, and the stench of spicy alcohol overtook her nose. Her water-filled eyes shot wide open whilst her small hands slapped back the bearded face that was hovering over her. He stumbled back, raising his hoarse, grumpy voice. She grabbed her small bag and jumped off the bench to run with as much speed as her legs could muster.

TUESDAY 27TH DECEMBER 2011

Instead of going back to work, Kris decided to pay his Aunt Louise a visit. He missed her and he needed someone to talk to about Lauren, even if it was none of his business. Kris drove at a perfect tranquil pace, slow enough to take in the journey and not so sluggish that he was annoying other drivers. He enjoyed having complete control and not being in a rush. The roads were clear whilst the intricately designed buildings drifted past him. He dropped the windows down and let the crisp London air swim through his lungs.

The speakers rang, pulling him from his reverie. "Clare. I'm driving. What is it? Why are you not at work?"

Her schoolgirl voice resonated through his Mercedes. "It's my day off and that's good! You're driving? Where are you going?" Kris swung his head back before manoeuvring his car into a side road, knowing what the next question was going to be once he answered.

∼

As Clare walked out of the house with a bounce in her step, her short brown beach waves ruffled in the air. Kris had known Clare ever since he could remember. From an irresponsible young girl, she had dipped into a dark world after Kelci had died. After a long time, she had finally discovered light to pull her out. This led her towards truth to renew her outlook on the world before her.

After the death of his parents, Kris had lost one of the most important people in his life; his wife, Kelci. Life had been kind to him when she reappeared to him as a ghost, with attached strings that needed to be unthreaded. With her help, he'd discovered that his uncle had been the one to murder his father by poisoning his drink on his birthday.

Kris had always found the death of his father to be unusual. The police brushed it aside, believing it was just a man that drank too much on his birthday, but Kris always knew his father wasn't a heavy drinker. He knew his uncle was many things. Jack had scammed money from his grandfather, attacked his mother and assaulted his wife; murder was not something he thought to add to the list. Kris had wanted Jack gone; throwing him behind bars at the time though never seemed to be a satisfying way to get rid of him. He couldn't bear placing the consequences of such an action on his aunt and his cousin.

Only his Aunt and he knew the truth about Jack and they always boxed it away whilst trying to build a new life with those around them. In the past few years after Kelci moved on, his aunt, his cousin Tim, Lauren and his in-laws were his support in creating a fulfilling life. He wasn't quite there; he just knew he was on the right road.

"Thanks Kris. All my friends are at work today. I was getting bored." Clare smiled.

He started the ignition and drove off without looking at her. "That's because it's a weekday. How come you got a day off?"

She shrugged. "Lazy day. Thought I should get an early weekend for all my hard work."

Kris moved his head side to side. "Lazy brat."

"Self-care is necessary! Besides, you can't talk." Kris stayed quiet and concentrated on the road ahead of him. "Did you miss Aunt Louise?" She tapped his shoulder lightly. "Awww, you did."

He rubbed his head. His mind was still seeing the caller ID from Lauren's phone. "Clare, please shut up." Clare remained quiet for a few seconds, then he saw her hand move towards the radio, "touch that and I'll leave you in the middle of this road!"

Clare puffed at the road ahead, crossing her arms like a schoolgirl that had just been told off for forgetting her homework. "What the hell did my sister see in you? You're so grumpy!"

Kris rolled his eyes. Clare always played loud music that would leave his ears thumping even after leaving the car. He wasn't having that on this day of all days, when his brain already felt like it was going to explode out of his head. Kris exhaled whilst steering his way into the quiet cul-de-sac and parked outside Aunt Louise's chic little house.

Kris got out of the car and jumped with a start after a loud bang; he clenched his jaw. "Will you watch how you slam my car door!"

Aunt Louise's house had become a comfortable home over the years. She placed beige carpet in the living room and bedrooms with fluffy brown cushions on all her sofas. Woodsy scented candles overtook your senses upon walking into the house, and plants were placed in the corners, wherever sunlight hit.

It seemed that Aunt Louise wasn't alone. "How come you haven't brought Lauren with you?" She asked when Kris entered.

Kris shifted his head forward, "because she's working, aunt Louise." She tutted and waved her hand in response. His cousin laughed. "I'm sorry, the girl wants pay, so she's going to have to work for it like every other person in this world!"

Clare narrowed her eyes, "so then, why aren't you working?"

"Same reason you're not." Kris tilted his head and met Clare's electric green eyes. His phone vibrated and he made his way into the kitchen.

Her voice was quiet and even. "You didn't like her." Kris didn't answer and he heard her exhale on the other side, "where are you?"

"Aunt Louise's. Shall I pick you up after work?"

"Please." He put the phone down and remembered the way he saw her outside his office all those years ago. All the blue and purple bruises on her face. The way she winced when he tried to help her up. The way she dragged her leg to the car. She had had no one. Everyone had left her. He dropped his head back and stared at the whirled white patterns on the ceiling that had yellow patches on it from the steam of the gas cooker.

He heard tapping and immediately lifted his head, "you going to tell me what's wrong then?" Aunt Louise asked. Kris rubbed the back of his neck. "You took time off work to come here, so you may as well talk."

Kris placed his hands in his pockets. "Do you know if Lauren is speaking to her mother?"

Aunt Louise sorted dried plates on the counter and made her way over to the sink. He walked over to his aunt to analyse her expression. She avoided his eyes by turning her face away. "I don't think this is any of my business Kris." Kris sighed. She then directed her eyes at him, "I do know her mother has tried to reach her."

Kris rubbed the base of his neck, about to answer until Tim walked in with a spring in his step. He halted and looked at them both with the chocolate-brown eyes he'd inherited from his mother. Kris reunited with his cousin a few years back after a lengthy gap. At the time, Kris had worried that Tim had inherited a small part of his father; this wasn't the case. If anything, he had completely absorbed his mother's cheerful personality. The only Dauni gene Tim seemed to have inherited was the perfectly neat, jet-black hair and nearly six-foot height that Kris also had. "Have I interrupted something?"

Aunt Louise pushed her shoulders back and put on a smile, "I forgot to ask you, how is Robyn doing in her job? You told me she'd been promoted to marketing executive."

Tim grinned, "why don't you just ask her?"

Aunt Louise blinked before walking out and leaving both Kris and Tim alone.

Tim grinned, leaning against the counter and picking on a bowl of grapes. Kris glanced towards the door. "Can I ask you something?"

Tim had come back to London with his girlfriend Robyn. She was a small, blonde haired, quiet girl, that Kris happened to find quite rude. The first time he'd met her, Lauren had attempted to strike up conversations on many occasions. Normally, shy people opened up to Lauren's personable personality, Robyn however continuously fired back blunt, one-word answers. It didn't bother Lauren, but it bothered Kris, because she did it to Aunt Louise too.

Tim shifted his eyebrows up and down at him before swallowing the red grape in his mouth, "you seem nervous." Kris placed his hands in his pockets and bit his tongue, "ask away."

Kris rubbed the base of his neck, "you're a decent guy."

"You're worrying me Kris." Kris tilted his head and rolled his eyes. Tim smiled and waved his hand from the top of his face to the bottom. His lips formed a straight line, "continue."

"You're a decent guy, outgoing, social, lively, so I was thinking..."

Tim tilted his head, "what do I see in Robyn?"

Kris's owl eyes popped open slightly, "I'm not offending you, am I? It's just, don't get me wrong, she's pretty and seems smart, but... she's the total opposite to you."

Tim chuckled before popping another grape into his mouth. "So, you're saying I'm ugly and dumb?" Kris rolled his eyes again, making Tim place his hands in his pockets. "She's interesting." Kris raised his eyebrows, "and complicated. And, in uni she made a change from most of the girls that sat in the lectures, flicking their hair around trying to get the lecturer's attention. I remember when I met her, she would hardly look at me, let alone talk to me."

"What a shocker." Tim narrowed his eyes at Kris. "Sorry. I shouldn't have said that." Kris defensively raised his hands, "Tim, I know it bothers you that she doesn't talk to anyone." Tim shrugged his shoulders and chewed on another grape. "Don't behave like you're okay with it. I've seen you arguing with her about it sometimes. Why are you with her if you don't like her?"

Tim snapped his head up, "I do like her."

"So then why aren't you stopping me and defending her?" Tim dropped his head in his hands.

Kris paused to pick up a grape. He peeled the skin off it before chewing it.

"I've always wanted my mum to speak about Robyn the way she does about Kelci." Tim said. Kris felt something drop in him. "I remember when I used to call. She used to go on and on about her. And when she wanted to speak to Robyn, I had to lie and make up some reason for her not being able to come to the phone. At that time, I didn't want to leave her. When it's just the two of us, she never stops talking but now…" Clare walked in and Tim dropped his head in fits of coughs. Kris stared at Tim watching his cheeks go slightly red.

Clare raised her eyebrows, "you alright there?" Tim nodded. She glanced between the two of them. "This is nice, isn't it? Aunt Louise relaxing and the two of you in here?"

"We're hardly cooking Clare, don't get excited." Tim said chewing on another grape.

Clare stuck her tongue out. "You know what would be so cool? If we had a cooking competition!"

Before Clare could involve him, he quickly glanced at his watch, "yeah Tim, you cook and I'll go pick up Lauren."

"So, Kris, you're basically chickening out." Clare laughed. She looked to Tim. "What about you? You must've cooked whilst you lived on your own." Kris burst out laughing and Clare turned her head between them confused. Tim began throwing grapes, making him sprint out of the kitchen.

Lauren was already standing in the large carpark when he arrived. He began manoeuvring the car around the moment she jumped in the passenger seat, "are you going to tell me why you're pissed off with me?" She looked at him, but his eyes remained fixed behind him to ensure he didn't hit into the brown-brick building. "Is it because you want me stop setting you up…?"

Kris shook his head, "why haven't you called your mother back?"

Lauren's brown eyes slowly widened like she'd just remembered the answer to a question, "how dare you!" Kris rolled his eyes as he realised her conclusion, "how dare you go through my calls! That's private!"

Kris placed his foot on the brake before he began driving through the car park exit. Lauren's eyes were wide and her jawline was clenched with her thin lips tight shut in a straight line. "I didn't look through your calls! She rang after you left the house this morning!"

"You're still completely crazy!" Lauren shouted waving her hands. He removed his foot from the brake and began slowly for the exit, "you're absolutely, ridiculously stupidly stupid!"

SMACK.

Kris immediately hit the brake. His eyes broadened at sight of the tall woman in front of him and Lauren's head spun around to the front window. The fierce angles of the lady's face made Kris's throat dry up. He felt a light thud in his chest, and he gulped. His owlish eyes squinted, realising that he recognised her.

Kris switched off the ignition to make his way out of the car. He blinked, becoming aware that he was staring at her. Her black hair was slightly shorter than how he remembered it and her circular, charcoal-black lined eyes darkened into the fading day. She hit the front of his car with her long fingers and Kris tried not to smile at the way her eyes were searing into him, "you could've killed my daughter!" She shouted. Kris stepped towards her with the intention of apologising, except no words left his slightly opened mouth. She smacked the car again. "Did you fake your driver's license!?"

"Kris!" Kris's eyes travelled down to the woman's arms and instantly his lips turned up. The young girl had become taller since the last time he saw her at the park and her long, jet-black hair was now a small bob that shaped her round face. Her brown eyes lit up with her dimpled, slightly pink, thick lipped smile.

Lauren approached the tall woman raising her hands slightly and apologising, "is your daughter okay?"

The daughter tugged at her mother's hand, "Mum don't you recognise him?!"

The woman's features sharpened on her square-shaped face. She pointed at Lauren, "*you* don't need to apologise!" She turned her finger towards Kris, "you do! You were the one driving and I don't understand what's so funny about this situation!"

Kris immediately placed his hand over his mouth, covering his smile. He couldn't comprehend why no words were leaving his mouth, even though he was thinking of the perfect apology. Reva began giggling; he quickly studied her again. He was surprised by how much Reva had grown up since he'd last seen her a few years back. As a ghost, Kelci had scared him out of the house before they had met after her death. Kris had decided to stay in a hotel for a while whilst Reva and her mother were also there. He used to find amusement in the way she had ran up and down the corridors entertaining herself.

Lauren faced him from the other side of the car with her eyes shooting lasers at him and her mouth agape. "Kris, apologise."

He set his eyes on the mother and he felt his thoughts drifting off into space again. He cleared his throat to speak before flinching upon hearing the loud smack of her hand hitting the bonnet of his Mercedes again. He hoped she hadn't dented his car. "Forget it. Complete idiot. Stupid man isn't going to apologise," she said in frustration. Kris instantly burst out laughing and Reva began giggling.

"Kris!" Lauren tapped the top of his car in attempt to get his attention. He was too busy watching the woman walking away. Reva circled around to wave at him. He threw his keys to Lauren and ran faster than the cars that were soaring past him on the busy road.

He stopped behind the woman, "excuse me." Reva spun around smiling at him, whilst her mother grabbed Reva's shoulders the way she did at the park. He fingers were long, and her nails were sharp. They reminded him of hands that would be shown on nail salon posters. Glisteningly oval varnished nails, long and delicate and ready to slit anything that bothered her. When she looked at him her pillowed lips were a firm, straight line and her grey eyes stabbed him. Kris ran his hand through his hair recognising a light thud in his chest again. He blinked his eyes away from her sharp features, trying to gather his thoughts. "I'm sorry." She dragged Reva back to walk off, but instead Reva released her hand and threw her arms around him. His arms flew up away from her, with a hint of confusion about how to react to her.

The mother rolled her eyes, "Reva!" Kris laughed watching her pull Reva back.

Reva shrugged her mother's hand away with a pout. "Mum, he isn't a stranger!"

Kris, surprised by his own movements, leant down in front of Reva onto one knee. Her mother placed her slender hands back on Reva's shoulders. He peeked up at the mother, "you've met me before." He focused his attention back to Reva, "it's just that your mother doesn't know me as well as you do. If you ever want to catch up, I'm over there." He pointed at his long black work building. "But don't go running off on your own. I don't think your mother's going to appreciate it."

Reva's brown eyes grew, "that's a very tall building." Her small mouth popped open in a round shape. She tilted her head up and then back down again, "Mum would you please calm down. This is Kris from the hotel." She jumped a little on the spot, "and you remember me!"

Kris chuckled, "how could I not remember you? You're the smallest chatterbox I know. And you've grown so tall!"

Reva's dimples gleamed back at him whilst her mother shifted slightly. "Sweetie. We need to go. I've got things to do."

Kris pulled himself onto his feet staring at the mother. "Sorry again." She put her head down and nodded whilst pulling Reva to walk away. A heaviness overtook him; a need to suddenly chase after them. With reluctance he walked back to his car, ensuring to check if there was a scratch or dent on it.

"What the hell was all that about?" Lauren asked, placing her mobile on her leg, "you didn't even shout at her the first, second or third time she hit your car. Instead you went all googly eyed at her. You didn't even shout at me when I tapped your car!"

Kris rolled his eyes, "googly." Kris was shutting out Lauren's talking so he could concentrate on not running anyone over whilst coming out the carpark exit. The workday was coming to an end, so the roads contained cars rushing past and getting stuck in traffic with drivers that were desperate to get home after a stressful day. Kris hastily tried to keep his eyes on the traffic. "Are you going to tell me why you've not called your mother back?" Lauren dropped her head down. "Lauren!"

Lauren bit her bottom lip. "I don't want to speak to her!"

Kris released a sigh before hitting the break at the traffic light. "Lauren, you know I never used to speak to my father that much. I was always angry with him, but if I had the chance to speak to him again, I would in a heartbeat." He lifted his foot off the brake, watching cars slowly move ahead in the traffic. Old buildings aligned along the road that had people rushing out of them, running for the train station nearby.

"No!" Lauren hit her leg, "it's my choice!"

Kris tried not to hit the brake too hard when he stopped again before the long line of cars in front of him. "What!?" Lauren rapidly nodded her head, "Lauren, this isn't about choice! And you know that!" Lauren breathed through her teeth, noticing the traffic pick up again.

"She left me by myself Kris!"

Kris sighed, before glancing at Lauren and then turning back to the queue of cars ahead of him. "Lauren, trust me I understand it's easier said than done, but you have to learn to let go. I'm not telling you to forget, but forgiveness is so important if you want to move forward in your life. This isn't just about your mother. Holding onto anger isn't healthy. Forgive for yourself, please."

Monday 21st February 1994

It was different. It wasn't like the stories she'd heard of or seen in films. There were a few of them. The one that kept asking her if she was okay was different from the rest. He never warned her; he comforted her. His voice was stern yet youthful. It reminded her of lotus flower; strong and beautiful.

It seemed that she may be a in a hotel. The room was large, with a television. There was no fridge though. Just a dressing table, mirror, television and a large double bed that was draped in cream-coloured covers. They gave her new clothes every day and someone always waited outside the bathroom whenever she showered or got changed in there. There was only one small window in the bathroom. A window she couldn't fit through even if she tried. Her bedroom had windows with only a view of endless fields. She didn't know where she was, or how far she was from her family. Her mind told her to keep resisting anything they said to her; but, a part of her wished she could be more cooperative, because she knew resistance wasn't going to take her far in this situation.

Tuesday 27th December 2011

Timothy stood outside his grey, uninviting flat door at twelve thirty in the morning. He hated coming back to his flat. Robyn's monotone voice did his head in. At one point in his relationship with her, he did love her. He had found her mysterious when they first met. He enjoyed the chase she gave. Every time he was rejected by her, he wanted to try and understand her more. He found her quietness and shyness to be cute, whereas now it was just mind numbing. It was hard to get a stimulating conversation out of her. It was even more ridiculous trying to do anything interesting with her. When they watched movies, she would show no sign of emotion. Especially, during comedy films, it would be awkward. Him laughing uncontrollably whilst she would just be staring at the television like it was a brand-new piece of technology that she'd never seen.

The many attempts of breaking up he'd made she never caught onto and over time it just became harder because he didn't want to hurt her feelings. She wasn't horrible or bad; her shyness and quietness was just too droning. The problem was that he still cared about her.

He'd come back from his mother's after an eventful evening. Clare had won a cooking competition that she had insisted on having. Before he began cooking, he saw an annoying message from Robyn informing him that she had gone home. She had given no reason. She'd just up and left. His mother questioned him, and he was forced to lie, saying she'd gone home because she was tired. She hadn't been to work all week and yet she was tired. He had no response to his mother's show of concern.

The only good thing about her leaving was that he didn't have to worry about Robyn actually being there; especially around Clare. Whenever Clare and Robyn were in the same room, he would feel like he was rolling down a steep hill. He had no intention of hurting Robyn, yet he knew he was developing feelings for Clare. Clare was a complete sunset in comparison to Robyn and her aura was like a breath of fresh air from the beach. Every time he was around her, he would get completely lost in her schoolgirl voice and summertime laugh.

The moment he realised what was happening he tried to avoid her presence completely. Of all things, it was mostly Kris's probable reaction that worried him most. Clare was Kris's sister in law. The whole idea would probably confuse him. Tim had picked up on how, like anyone else, Kris was protective of his family, and though Tim and Kris were cousins, Kris's relationship with Clare was stronger.

Tim slammed the door behind him. The state he found his small flat in wasn't what he was expecting.

Smashed glass was all over his brown carpet. His small table was tipped to the side and his glass fruit bowl was scattered everywhere. Tim made a frightened attempt to move forward. Glass cracked underneath his foot and he took a deep breath: "Robyn!" He walked further into the room. *Crack. Crack. Crack.* His beige sofa had been torn right down the middle. He opened his room door and it was empty. The drawers had been left open. The mirror had been shattered. There were dents in his walls. There were drops of blood on the dressing table.

His breathing scattered upon nearing the box bedroom. Blood covered the handle. He swallowed. His heart was racing, and a heavy brick was weighing his chest down. He stepped into the bedroom slowly. He heard heavy breathing. The room was dark, so he slowly raised his hand up to the light switch. He was preparing himself for whatever he may see next.

Robyn was nowhere to be seen. Blood was splattered on parts of the floor. The room was stuffy. He wondered if his flat radiators had been left on full blast the whole day. He took a deep breath and walked to the opposite side of the bed.

He felt himself fall into the ground beneath him. His mind attempted to fathom the sight before him. He ran up to Robyn and tried to squeeze his thick fingers between her neck and the wire she had wrapped around herself. She hissed. He could feel her hands pull the ends of the wire further. He tried not to look at the blood on her arms and clothes as he struggled to pick at the wire squeezed around her neck. "Robyn, let go!" Tim couldn't think of anything else to do. He threw his hand over her cheek and she fell lifelessly to the floor. Tim quickly drew the wire away from her skin. If she wasn't crying, he would've thought she was dead already.

He stepped closer to her and heard her hiss, "stay away from me." If his hands weren't shaking, he wouldn't believe he was scared. She pulled herself up from the floor with her eyes shooting at him. The stench of her soaked in blood burned his eyes. He wondered if she even knew what she was doing or what was happening. Within seconds, Tim saw the lamp flying towards him. He rushed out of the way. "GET LOST!" Robyn was in front of him shouting. Her hair seemed to have been pulled out at all ends. Her face was dry and covered with tiny red spots. "GO THEN!"

"Robyn, have you been possessed or something? What the hell is wrong with you?!"

She yanked at the ends of her hair and he drew back from her. "Timmy, I don't know. Why don't you go and ask your two-faced cousin!" Tim stared at her. Seconds went by and he was still speechless. All this because she'd heard the conversation he had with Kris in the afternoon. Anyone else would've just simply shouted and interrogated him, instead Robyn had torn his whole flat apart along with herself. He stumbled out of the room.

He took a deep breath and said, "to make it clear Robyn, we're over."

Robyn followed behind him as he sped to the front door. The moment he twisted the door handle he jumped at the sound of a picture crashing against the wall. He exhaled quickly, shutting the door behind him with a ringing slam, still hearing her screams resonating through the hallway.

Tim finally slid into his car, dropping his head back. Though this was the first time he'd seen her trying to take her life, he knew he couldn't deal with drama. Every week she would have a teenage tantrum and he'd had enough of it. He checked the time and it was coming up to one in the morning. This situation was so humiliating.

Whilst turning the wheel, one thought tugged at his mind: what if Robyn does kill herself? If she does do something to herself it would be on his conscience. However, she wasn't ten. She had to be the grown woman that she was to take care of herself.

Wednesday 7th September 1994

Robyn's head rested on her jumper. She had been in the carriage all day. People had walked in and out, staring at her because they perceived her to be a young girl with nothing. At this point she was. All she owned was a small bag of clothes. People stared at her scruffy hair that hadn't been washed in weeks. She'd been jumping from train to train for a while, because it was the only shelter she could find that didn't include people creeping up on her. Her legs felt like iron and jelly at the same time. She felt them pulsing along the train seats that smelt like dust. She had no idea where the central line had stopped, so she had no clue where she was. She was just glad that the train tracks weren't screeching, the sound screamed in her head. She needed silence.

Twelve midnight brought stillness, making her eyelids drop.

Tuesday 27th December 2011

Kris rubbed his eyes after putting the phone down on his cousin and made his way down the stairs to the front door. He jumped back, blinking at the state in front of him. Tim walked in and approached the staircase. Kris quickly swung the door shut and blocked his cousin, who was standing confused wearing blood-soaked clothes. Kris was aware that Tim was his father's son, so if he was coming across unwelcoming, he didn't care. He didn't need more drama in his life. He eyed the blood on Tim's sleeves. "I'm sorry, just tell me, have I let a killer through my front door?" He said, trying hard to sound light-hearted. Tim rolled his eyes and walked past Kris to make his way up the stairs.

With the assumption that Tim was going to be staying the night, he left clothes in the guest room for him and then made his way downstairs. He poured himself a brandy and then sat down on the sofa waiting. He rubbed the base of his neck, thinking about what Tim had done. He was his father's son after all. Was he being judgemental? It was wrong to judge someone based on who they were related to, wasn't it? He scrutinized the picture of him with his parents. Then again, he wouldn't want to be judged as a complete workaholic just because of his father.

"I can't even imagine what's going through your head right now." Kris swivelled from behind the sofa to see Tim walk down the stairs completely fresh in his grey pyjamas.

"Why don't you help yourself to a drink and then explain to me what happened."

Tim poured himself a vodka and then sat down next to him before explaining about what happened with Robyn when he got home. How her arms and clothes were covered in blood. How his flat was a complete frightening mess and how she threw a lamp at him. When Tim finished, Kris didn't have any words. How could someone try to take their own life? He knew suicide was a common cause of death and he never understood how people were capable of actually doing that to themselves. It was just like killing another person, how does one have such strength to commit to such an act?

"She could be killing herself and it would be my fault for not being there for her."

Kris clicked his tongue, "no, she is fully grown woman with a fully-grown brain. She's not your child." Tim chewed the inside of his mouth whilst staring at the floor. Kris rolled his eyes, "seriously Tim, there are so many women out there in the world, could you not pick a normal, sane one?" Kris rubbed his hand through his hair, "ring her."

Kris made his way to the bar to refill his glass. The thought of someone trying to take their own life made him shudder. He couldn't ever handle going back to the situation that Tim had today. He wondered what made her so angry. What pushed her to do something like that? Kris walked back to the sofa and waited until Tim placed the phone back down. "Has she done this before?"

Tim exhaled, "not that I know of."

"So, in other words, she may have."

"I've seen her doing strange things though," Tim said, "she scratches her arm," Kris pushed his head back, smiling lightly, "you don't understand. She's oblivious to it. Like, if she's staring at a screen, she'll scratch her arm until it bleeds. Sometimes she does it while eating. She just stares at her food and scrapes her arm. It's just crazy. It's not normal." Kris stared at Tim with his mouth agape. How could someone do something like that and be unaware of the pain they were causing themselves? "And Kris, her mood swings! They're bloody mad! Like a couple of weeks ago, she was absolutely silent around Mum's and then when we came home, she was all jumpy and hyper. And then when we sat down and watched a film, she was back to scraping the skin off her arm."

Tim put his head in his hands and Kris hit the side of his leg, "Tim, take her to her parents."

Tim rubbed his face then lifted his head up. "She hasn't got any." Kris squinted his eyes and sighed deeply. Tim interlocked his fingers, "her father left her when she was a child and her mother... well, Robyn never mentions her."

"So, you don't know what happened between her and her mother? What about siblings?"

Tim shrugged and Kris raised his eyebrows, "so, she may have siblings."

Tim shrugged his shoulders again, "I asked her a couple of times when we first met and she would ignore the question and when I tried to push a little further for an answer she kind of went a little..." Kris tilted his head searchingly at him, "let's just say that I thought it would be best not to ask again."

Kris rolled his eyes. "Tim it's just occurred to me, do you know anything about this woman?"

Tim's eyes shot open. "Of course I do!"

"Doesn't seem like it. How many years were you with her and it never occurred to you to ask her about her mother and find out properly if she has siblings?"

Tim squinted his eyes, "I just thought we are the ones in the relationship so it wouldn't matter."

Kris bit his lip, "you're right, you both are the ones in the relationship so if *her* past is taking a toll on the current relationships then it matters to understand why it's taking a toll." Tim sighed and Kris continued, "some way, you need to find out about her family because I think that is what is affecting her, and maybe they could help her." Kris raised his hand stopping Tim from defending himself, "figure it out. Because if you don't want to help her, she needs somebody." Tim's lips pursed before throwing back the rest of his drink.

∼

Tim sat downstairs staring at the wall. All he could think was that he shouldn't have left Robyn on her own. She was fully capable of taking her own life. How could he be so stupid? By not staying with her after her attempt at strangling herself, he had just shown her that he had no care in the world for her. Kris was right though; he had to put his foot down and force her to talk about her family.

Robyn always evaded the subject of her family whenever he questioned her about them. Eventually, he stopped asking her. He realised the hard way that she didn't like it.

Tim should've walked away from this situation when he had the chance. Now that he had sunk in too deep, how could he walk away? What type of person would that make him?

∼

The air was boiling hot, but Robyn felt awfully nippy from a chill that run through her. Her head was banging hard like a hammer against a nail being pushed into a brick wall. Her arms were full of blood. Her hair was soaking wet. Robyn had been frozen in this position for hours, nonetheless her heart was racing fast like she'd run a marathon. Her jaw had been aching for hours. Water didn't stop pouring from her eyes no matter how much they burnt. Her pulsing body lay on the bed staring into complete darkness.

A shiver ran through the room again and she heard someone call out her name. Her head lifted slowly off the pillow towards the direction of the noise causing a thumping pain at the side of her brain that made her squint her eyes. Something tugged her head lightly back down to the pillow and she gasped, feeling a cold hand stroke her head. The chilliness awakened her insides even though the touch was soft and comforting. She recognised it from university. The subtle cold contact used to help her eyes rest.

Friday 28th December 2011

Kris lugged his legs down the stairs whilst yawning and rubbing his eyes. He felt like a drained rug from the lack of sleep. He opened the door and Lauren stood wearing a bright lilac jumper than was littered with small, pink flowers. Lauren tutted when seeing Kris covering his eyes. He stepped back to let her in as she said, 'you look awful.'

She shut the door behind her, "and you're not wearing that to work."

She glanced down at her jumper, "it's just for the journey. It's cold. And besides, what's it to you?" She shrugged before halting on the way to the kitchen, "why is Tim sleeping on your sofa?"

Kris stepped closer to his beige sofa, seeing Tim with his arms hanging off the edge. He smacked his cheek lightly, making Tim mumble. Lauren giggled then made her way into the kitchen. Kris smacked Tim across the cheek a little harder and he jumped up. Kris tried to keep a straight face even though he found his cousin's confused state funny, "you know, without sounding big headed, I have more than one spare bedroom in this house."

Tim rubbed his hair and blinked rapidly before getting up and scanning the house like he'd just landed on another planet. "I've got to get to work."

Kris shook his head, "go back upstairs and sleep. Go in a little later." Tim rubbed his eyes. "Tim..."

Tim shot his eyes at him, "you've had the same amount of sleep."

"I haven't come home to a nutty girlfriend." Kris grabbed the cup of coffee Lauren left for him when he walked into the kitchen. He held on to it protectively, watching Lauren's eyes on him in anticipation of an explanation. "Let's just put it this way, if this relationship ends you can play matchmaker."

"Don't think I need to. I think he's already found his match in Clare." Kris's head snapped up and his eyes widened. He placed the mug down on the counter, hoping he heard wrong. "What?" He rubbed his hands through his hair and exhaled.

"You don't have an issue with Tim being interested in Clare, do you?"

"He can't like Clare. He doesn't like Clare." He dropped his hands. *Jack's son can't like Clare.* A thread began weaving in the midst of his chest, "how can you say that?"

Lauren giggled. "Kris, don't tell me you haven't noticed how Tim looks at her as if he's just been starstruck by some celebrity. Didn't you notice him yesterday?" Kris placed his hands against the counter. Lauren analysed him, "you actually have an issue. Why?"

He wanted to believe that Lauren was seeing things – she had a knack for seeing everything so clearly though. She picked up on stories in his office that no one else could. "Whatever. It's just not going to happen." Kris tried to keep an even tone when speaking, "it can't happen." She blinked as her brown eyebrows pulled together. "You have work."

Lauren chewed on her bottom lip, focusing her stare on her coffee. She placed her finger on the edge of the mug tracing it, "I actually wanted to know what yesterday was about?" Kris blinked. "Normally when someone beats your car up you have a fit, instead your eyes went droopy as if she was Toodles."

Kris felt heat rise up in his cheeks, "who on earth is Toodles?"

Lauren waved her hand, "how do you know her or the little girl?"

"Do you remember that hotel I stayed in a while back?" Kris picked his mug back up and sipped.

"Wow. She's got very good memory," Kris nodded, and Lauren's lips went up, "so what you going to do?"

"About what?" Lauren tilted her head to the side, squinting her eyes at him. He rubbed the base of his neck and placed his mug back down on the counter, "you have work."

Lauren huffed, picking up her bag. She turned for the door then rotated on the spot back round again, "listen Kris. I've noticed you don't like Tim's Dad." Kris gulped, placing his mug down on the counter, "you stiffen at the sound of his name. But for whatever reason, don't take that out on Tim. He's one of the good ones."

"It's not Tim that I've got the issue with. It's his father. I don't want Clare anywhere near him."

Lauren walked back towards Kris, "Clare isn't a toddler Kris. She has her own smarts. She doesn't like him either." Kris exhaled and rubbed the back of his neck. "Anyway, I don't know why you're stressing. Tim is with Robyn right now." Kris sighed whilst Lauren tucked her hair behind her ears, "either way, whatever happens between them is none of your business."

"It's my business." Lauren rolled her eyes. Kris blinked, attempting to bury the story his mother had told him in the back of his mind and tried to wipe out Jack's words about his wife. Before he could help himself, like a running tap he blurted out his mother's story of how Jack had attacked her in his father's office. How Jack was the cause of his parent's separation and how he had also assaulted Kelci during his father's birthday.

THURSDAY 4TH AUGUST 1994

The air was sizzling around her, making her hair stick to her face like a heavy-soaked cloth. She hated this emotion. Her heart was drumming in her ears. She should get up and open a window; her joints hurt though. How could she move? Pain ran through her like a house on fire. In the back of her neck. In her shoulders. The sides and middle of her stomach. Her legs. The bottom of her feet. Even her wrists and hands. All loaded with a heavy pain. Her shoulders and the top of her arms were a different pain though. Sharp and bolting from the weight of her thoughts. Her head moved back and forth without her permission.

So many questions. They were sprinting through her mind. Why did they hate her so much? Why did they treat her so cruelly? What had she done to them? Was she really such a freak? Wasn't she clever? Why didn't she resemble Estella? Why couldn't her mother be her mum? Why couldn't her father be here with her? Why didn't her father love her? Why did Tanya stop speaking to her? The teachers all spoke to her weirdly, why? Why? Why? Why? Why? She needed the questions to go away.

SMACK. She felt the cold wall at the back of her head. They wouldn't go; it wasn't working. She let her head swing back into the wall again and felt nothing except a lingering coolness. The questions wouldn't go.

"Please stop." She whispered to herself. Tears flooded down her cheeks. Pain was absent from the lump that was forming at the back of her head. SMACK. She glimpsed downwards. Where did the blood come from? SMACK. More tears ran down her cheeks.

BANG. BANG. BANG. Her eyes popped open at the door. Nayla was screaming her name. She didn't want to answer. She wanted her to leave her alone. The noises were getting louder. She still didn't want to answer.

"Robyn, get out the flipping bathroom!" She slowly climbed off the marble floor with an intense pain vibrating through her body.

She unlocked the door and waited for the lecture. Her sharp-faced mother stared at her with her small brown eyes and angular jaw clenched. Robyn stood fixing her large wet eyes at her mother's dark blue flowery top. Robyn watched her mother's eyes whiz around the bathroom. "M..."

Robyn's mother stepped forwards, searing her stare into her more deeply, making her gulp, "don't 'mum' me! All I could hear was banging!"

Nayla's eyes scanned the inside of the bathroom; they widened in dismay at the amount of water covering the white tiles. Robyn heard a door click and immediately she dropped her face. She didn't want her sister looking at her like this. It'll only give her more of a reason to freak shame her. "Mum what's with all the... Robyn, your arm. What happened to your arm?"

Her mother pointed at the bathroom, "I've had enough of you!" Nayla shoved her face right in front of Robyn's and the scent of the rich, woodsy perfume made her swallow. "This ends here."

Estella forced her way between Robyn and Nayla. "Mum stop it! You're making her cry!"

Nayla lifted herself up and pointed at Robyn, "*I'm* making her cry." Nayla screamed, "what about what she has done to us?!"

Robyn stood there with tears streaming down her face, trying to comprehend the last time she had spoken or interacted with her mother and sister. What had she done? What had she done to upset them? What had she done to upset everyone?

Estella shouted over her mother's shrieking, "Mum, she hasn't done anything to us!"

Robyn wanted her bed. She wanted to be unconscious. She didn't want to deal with all that was happening. She walked away so that she could get away from the shouting. She halted when

Nayla pushed Estella to the side. Robyn suddenly let out a hurtling scream. "I don't have to deal with you!" Nayla shouted with a load of Robyn's hair in her hand. Robyn's screams did nothing to help the agony of being hauled down the stairs by her hair.

Estella grabbed Robyn's arm, "Mum let go of her! Please, you're hurting her!"

All Robyn could do was yell and hold onto her head. Strands of hair were pricking out from her skin. Nayla finally let go when she shoved her out of the front door and held Estella's short arm back from reaching out for her. "I don't have to have you under my roof any longer. You're old enough to take care of yourself. I've done my bit!"

The brown door slammed in her face and that was the last that she saw of her mother. Robyn scanned the street, blinking with tears in her eyes, trying to figure out what just happened. She knew her mother would be angry, but she wasn't expecting to be thrown out onto her front porch. She dragged her feet back a few strides and felt needles prickling into the insides of her neck.

Waterfalls began again. She slumped herself on the dirty ground. Her head burnt. She could hear yelling from the house, and she covered her ears.

The volume of sounds reduced. Her sight blurred. Everything went black.

MONDAY 12TH SEPTEMBER 1994

She had been sleeping on the train for a few nights. She would make a habit of switching trains every now and then so that she wasn't caught at any point. Other than that, she only left the station when it was empty for the sake of stealing food from somewhere. The stations were normally dark, dirty and usually smelt like filthy rain. The nastiness surrounding her would make her nose tingle and would sometimes make her lay awake on the train without gaining any sleep. Sleep deprivation was beginning to get to her, because her migraines would make small noises seem like fireworks.

Today she was going to aim for fast food stalls. Leaving the station in a rush, she felt the crisp wind blowing through the underground, so she pulled her jumper out of her small carrier bag. The cold was pricking at her bruised skin and all she could think of was snuggling into a consoling bed. However, right now this wasn't the case; she had to focus on her present.

Out of nowhere, her throat was grabbed by the neck of her jumper, making her release a wailing scream. Her back hit against the grimy station wall. She felt something sharp and her voice bottled. A person in a black hoodie and scarf covering his face snatched her bag from her hand and ran. She couldn't stop her shaking legs. Her body crumbled to the floor whilst she let out a scream in her small hands.

Friday 5th August 1994

Something was hitting her and she could feel an ache moving inside as she was being shoved back and forth. She needed it to stop. She squeezed her eyes tighter. "Robyn, get up." Her eyes opened slightly, and her hand flew to her head. The events of the previous night came swamping back to her. Something smelt damp. She sighed, placing her hands on her legs, which felt like iron rods. Estella helped her up from the ground. "Here." Estella held out a bottle of water that she didn't take, "I've literally just crept out of the house, I stuffed all the clothes I could find into any bag I could find." Robyn's eyes narrowed watching her sister fumble and talk, "I don't want to be caught. Otherwise Mum is going to place my head on a golden platter. I've called one of my friends. And she said you can stay…"

A fire blazed in Robyn's stomach, "your friends!"

Estella's head moved back, "well I don't see any of your friends here."

Robyn brushed her greasy hair out of her face, which smelt of sweat and dampness, "Estella, why are you helping me?! You can't call me a freak one minute and the come running to my rescue the next! I don't need you and I definitely don't need any of your flipping stuck up brainless friends!"

Estella blinked whilst knotting the carrier bag in her hand.

"Robyn, you're my sister. I'm going to be there for you. We fight and argue, that's how sisters are supposed to be."

Robyn snickered and clapped, "oh wow, that's a great act. Well done. You should go into movies, trust me you've got the attitude for it. Your amazing 'I-care-about-you-no-matter-what' routine will take you far."

Estella's bottom lips quivered whilst the bag dropped from her hands, "I've always cared about you!"

"So then where were you when that witch of a mother of mine left me in the house for nearly two weeks on my own whilst you both were off on holiday? I didn't even know you were on holiday until you walked back through door!" Robyn's voiced trembled, "or what about every single birthday of mine?!" Robyn felt every ounce of hatred crawling through her mouth. She walked up to Estella and met her eyes, "why have me and keep me if you don't want me? Don't you think I would've been happier if I had a mother and father that actually remembered that I was alive? My mother doesn't even have to bother saying it to me because I know she thinks that my existence was a serious fault in this world."

"Shut up!" Estella staggered back. Robyn stared at her sister's face, which was drenched in tears: "so fine, I'm not the best sister, but I am still your sister and I'm not going to let you sleep on this filthy ground all night!"

"But my mother lets me!" Robyn sprinted to the front door. She swung her leg at it. Her hands burned from smacking the brown painted wood. She wanted her mother to come running out to her. Telling her that it was a mistake. That she didn't mean to throw her out. To tell her that all that happened wasn't supposed to happen. "Mum!" She felt arms being pulled back, "let go of me!" Estella dragged her back by the arm until she finally gave up. The greasy smell overtook her senses, making her drop her shoulders. She swallowed, staring at her sister.

Robyn knew she should feel sorry for her, and she wanted to feel for her sister; nevertheless, she felt nothing. "Cry," she said as Estella's red eyes bore into her with water continuing to stream down her cheeks, "keep crying, it doesn't get you anywhere. As much as the tears come spilling out, as much as your chest just yearns to explode, as much as your breathing scatters, it doesn't change anything that happens around you. Trust me, every day that has gone past, I craved for a little bit of love from my family, and for every craving, I cried and as much as I cried, nothing changed. In fact, I can tell you that it just makes things worse. Where I'm standing now is proof."

Robyn scrutinised the house. Every day after school she hated walking into this house. A dirty remark from her sister, a horrible word from her mother or just the simple fact of not being noticed always set her to waterworks. This wasn't a home for her. The prettiness of this house was a disguise for the hell that her mother truly made out of it.

Life is given to a person so that they live. It's an opportunity to revel in happiness. So then what was the reason for her being given life, if she'd never been given the chance to be happy? She stared at the small white house and then back at her sister stumbling back from apprehension. This position she was in right now, could be that opportunity. She should leave and try to find happiness. Her brain shouted at her legs to turn around and walk away. She picked up the blue carrier bag that her sister brought out before dragging her feet off the house porch. "Robyn!" Her sister was behind her. "Robyn, where are you going to go?"

Robyn examined her sister's worried face: "go back to your mother Estella." She had no idea what her next step was.

Monday 3${}^{\text{RD}}$ October 1994

The coffee shop was alive with people at twelve thirty all the way through to two o'clock. Lunch brought people swarming in like ants making Robyn so overwhelmed that she felt reduced to crumbs. She tried to stay focused on the way her manager gave her orders, alongside cleaning the equipment in the café, clearing out the back storage and cleaning the toilets. The process made her feel like she had spiders crawling on her skin and at times she wanted to walk out. She had to continuously keep reminding herself that this job kept her off the streets and away from creepers approaching her on benches. All the little money she earned went towards a dingy hotel that kept a roof over her head. The food wasn't what she hoped it to be, even for a low budget hotel, but it gave her a bed for the endless nights and water to remove the dirt from her skin. The important part was that this wasn't going to be for long. She had been accepted into university and was due to begin in a few weeks. She placed the chairs on freshly wiped down tables to continue mopping. She beamed, knowing she had done something right.

Part Two

Monday 9th January 2012

Kris had managed to get through all the revenue sheets of his businesses over the past week. He exited all the tabs with a wide grin. Stepping back from his ventures was one of the best decisions he'd ever made in life. His only regret was that he hadn't done it sooner.

Tim had been staying round his house ever since he had left Robyn. Kris had no desire to raise the subject of Clare with him. He hadn't confided everything in Lauren, with what he had told her she was very shocked. She advised that he should tell Clare only if there was a reason to do so. However, he was reluctant to open the lid of a toppling jar that he closed a very long time ago.

Tim was unaware of his father's messes and Kris respected his Aunt's wishes of keeping it that way. Nonetheless, it didn't stop him from leaving the room every time Tim mentioned his father. Every time Jack's name was stated, the night of his father's birthday would come crawling back inside his mind and overtake his thoughts. He would feel Kelci's trembling small body beside him again and see Jack's large arm snaking up to her neck. Jack's words from the last time he met him would ring in his ears and he would resist telling Tim to shut up about his revolting father.

He would bite his tongue, thinking about Kelci. She had seen the light the moment he had managed to gain Jack's confession of how he murdered his father. This confession was Kelci's unfinished business. He was meant to find out the truth. Before she left him, he had promised her he would try to be happy. It was a promise that he planned on sticking to, no matter how difficult it got.

The sound of a knock pulled him from his thoughts of Kelci. He saw Ayva standing by the door and wondered if the office had forced her to play a game of truth and dare. She turned behind her, "come in sweetie, he's here." Kris hauled himself from his chair and made his way to the other side of his desk. Reva came jumping from behind Ayva and wrapped her arms around him.

Kris looked at Ayva with his eyes open and hands up. Ayva smiled, "they called from downstairs reception. Apparently, she just kept asking for you." Kris rubbed his head. "I didn't want to turn her away. She was on her own."

Kris nodded and bent down in front of Reva, "Reva, where's your mother?" He glanced at the clock and it was only coming up to the three. "Your mum thinks you're in school." Reva's brown eyes dropped when Ayva left the office. "Give me her number." She raised her nose and Kris said sternly "Reva, your school's going to ring your mother and then your mother is going to panic." Reva shook her head and crossed her arms. "I need your mum's number." She pretended to be interested in the sights Kensington had to offer from the window and Kris said again, "Reva."

She shot her brown eyes at him and her lips dropped. "She's a hairdresser at Ella's." Kris rubbed his head whilst researching for local hairdressers on the internet. *A person that thinks their child is missing isn't good,* he thought. Reva placed herself down on the chair and slouched, "she wouldn't let me come!"

"Reva we may be friends, but to your mother I'm a complete stranger!"

Reva pushed herself forward on the chair. "How would we have met then?"

Kris dialled the number he had found before placing the phone to his ear listening to the bell, "we met randomly after so many years and that was such a coincidence. I guess that we just hope for more coincidences. What's your mum's name?"

She chewed the inside of her lip, "Adara Fields."

Within a few moments a woman's voice that sounded like she had a sore throat answered. Kris hung up the phone after giving them his location. He crossed his hands on the desk, watching her taking in the room around her, and asked "do you want some juice or something?"

She continued moving her head around the room after shaking it. "My mum's going to come in shouting. She won't stop hugging me for the next couple of weeks because she's going to think I'm going to disappear into thin air." Kris laughed, suddenly thinking of his mother, but Reva continued, "…she's very annoying. Ever since we stopped moving around, she screams so much more when she's scared." He stared at her. "We used to move to different hotels all the time, and then my grandmother came, and we finally got to stay in a house." Kris blinked and then just nodded his head in thought. "Do you like working here? It looks very boring. On TV they show all these men behind desks and they look so bored and unhappy."

Lauren walked in with her head in a sheet of paper, disrupting Kris's chuckle. "Kris you didn't sign..." Her eyes lifted, "oh, sorry."

"Lauren, this is Reva and Reva, Lauren is one of the reasons why work never gets boring." Lauren placed the paper on his desk in front of him.

Reva grinned at Lauren and she smiled back. "Hi Reva." Lauren tilted her head a little, "wow, Kris, did you just say something nice about me?" She looked at Reva, "he never normally says nice things about me."

Reva's giggle stopping Kris from rolling his eyes, "are you two married?"

"No!" Kris and Lauren said simultaneously.

Kris's eyes settled on the document that confirmed that he was buying the building he'd been after from Gal. His eyes narrowed slightly, bringing the paper closer to him to read. He rubbed the base of his neck, seeing that she had dropped her price.

Lauren was bent down in front of Reva, "I've worked at so many places and sometimes the jobs are fun, but it's not always about the work. It's about the people. The people here are really nice, and we all get along so well. Do you want me to introduce you to my friends?" Reva diverted Kris's attention from the paper when she jumped up to remove her black furry coat and place her red school bag back down. He watched them walk out of the room.

Kris clicked his tongue and signed the paper before leaving it on the corner of his desk. It took Gal a week to agree and he was surprised she did. Ayva walked in with the sound of her tapping heels, "Kris, I think that little girl's mum's here."

"Just send her in," he said. Ayva stepped back, but he called again, "Ayva," she turned, and he pointed at the document, "send this back to Kallahan straight away please."

Ayva picked up the document, exclaiming "she finally gave in!"

She stroked her ponytail as she took in the contents of the paper. Kris focused on her and his lips turned up slightly, "how did you know?"

"I saw the email and forwarded it to you and Lauren this

morning. I think she saw it before you." She pointed at the paper and stepped towards the door, "I'll get this done." Kris watched her walk out.

Kris felt his mouth go dry when he saw Adara walk in a few seconds later. She had her hands in her black coat. Her large, charcoal eyes scanned the room the same way her daughters did. Kris's eyes fixated on the way her tall length was reserved; making it clear that she wasn't letting anyone into her personal perimeter. Her fiery demeanour knocked his breath away completely. Kris gulped, then pointed at the chair, "sit down. She's coming."

Adara continued standing. "Thanks so much for calling me." He noticed the whites in her eyes were faintly red and her thin eyeliner was slightly smudged at the tops of her eyelids. She pushed her hair back behind her ears, which were pierced with silver studs. "I'm so sorry about this whole thing, she…"

"Adara, it's okay. I did say for her to come. Sit down. Your daughter's perfectly safe. Do you want a glass of water or something?"

"Yeah but…" Her long lashes fluttered, "it's Kris, right?"

He nodded, "yeah, Kris Dauni." She squinted, and her head tilted slightly, studying his features. He felt his face go slightly red, making him exhale and stare down at his desk. The silence broke when Reva came running in with Lauren behind her.

Adara dropped to her knees and grasped her daughter into a hug. "Mum, I'm fine. I have two arms, two hands, two legs and my face!" Lauren covered her smile. Kris tried not to laugh whilst they watched Adara tighten her grip, "Mum!"

Adara let go and exhaled. She straightened out Reva's hair, muttering "sorry, my child leaves during school hours and all I can think is that she's being held hostage somewhere out there in the middle of nowhere."

Reva stomped her foot, "well I'm not. I'm fine," she shoved her head forward so that she was face-to-face with her mother, "and safe!"

Adara closed her eyes, taking in a deep breath she pushed her shoulders back and lifted herself up, "coat and school bag," she said. Reva's shoulders dropped, "now." Adara's large eyes focused in on Kris. He quickly wiped the large grin off his face, "thank you so much for taking care of her and calling." Kris shook his head. "The truth is though, I really don't understand why my daughter's attached to you."

Lauren burst out giggling. Reva ran around the desk, and Kris took her into his arms to receive her hug. "I hope we have another coincidence." Kris smiled, letting go of her and then watched them walk out.

"See, there you go again," Lauren was narrowing her eyes at him. She twirled her finger at his face, "looking at her the way Tom looks at Toodles." Kris dipped his eyes to his desk, "you like her."

"I hardly know her, Lauren," he said sitting back down on his chair, "and you've got things to do."

Lauren puckered her closed mouth side to side in contemplation before leaving the room.

Monday 16th January 2012

Kris laid his keys down on the side table and immediately felt the warmth radiating from the marble. He removed his jacket and hung it in the cloakroom, before walking into the kitchen. He prepared himself a plate of pasta and made his way to the living room. His eyes broadened at the sight in front of him. He froze at the door, staring at Clare sitting crossed legged and huddled into Tim, who had his arm around her. A heaviness formed in Kris's chest and he took a deep breath in the hopes that it would lighten. Clare averted her eyes away from the television. "Kris," Tim's head snapped in his direction with his pupils shimmering wildly. "Why are you standing at the door?"

Tim brought his arm back to move away slightly and Clare glanced at him. Kris's focus remained on Tim when he spoke: "Clare, what you doing here?"

Tim was a commercial designer and didn't normally finish work until five thirty. It took some time for Tim to get a job after he had finished university and once he finally got his job, he loved it and was promoted very quickly. He normally worked late, so Kris was wondering what he was doing home so early.

Clare dropped her legs down from the sofa, "Tim invited me."

Kris breathed deeply, walking into the living room. The doorbell rang, giving Tim a start. Kris bit the inside of his lip as he rolled his eyes, placing his plate down on the table.

"Robyn!" Tim had refused to see Robyn since he had broken up with her. Clare ran from the sofa to shut the door and then placed her ear against it. Kris waved his hands questioningly. Clare's lips twitched and he shrugged before placing his ear against the door. "Robyn, I did say we're over."

"I'm sorry." Robyn's light voice staggered.

"You're obviously not if you came here, of all places." Kris's eyebrows raised. They went quiet for a while until Tim broke the silence. "Do you have any brothers or sisters?"

"Why are you asking me that?" Robyn's voice was venomous. There was a few seconds' silence and Kris hoped his mother's valued possessions weren't going to be the casualty of their conversation. "Just one sister. Estella and I had an argument, we haven't spoken since."

"How many years have they been together, and he asks her that now?" Clare whispered. Kris just shrugged, twisting away from the door; he'd heard the name Estella before.

He placed his ear back to the door. "You already know about my father, and my mother's dead." Her voice was frighteningly icy. Kris heard the amount of hatred in the word 'dead'. She was lying. "Where are all these questions coming from?" Kris stepped away from the door again, rubbing his jaw. The name Estella was still ringing in his head. It bothered him that he couldn't remember. He then heard her shout.

Tim hissed, "Robyn, this isn't my house so keep your volume down! And, you're right, this isn't my business anymore."

"Tim, I'll talk to whoever you want me to talk to." Robyn's crying could be heard through the doors. Clare scrunched her eyes and bit her bottom lip.

"Speaking to my family shouldn't be an obstacle."

There were a few seconds silence before Tim said, "I think you should leave."

"Tim, I don't like being alone."

Kris watched Clare back away from the door, picking at her

fingers. Her eyes remained on the floor. After a few seconds the front door slammed. "You guys can come out now."

～

In the family room, Clare sat next to Tim on the sofa, watching him bind his fingers together. Kris wanted Clare to leave. He didn't like the amount of comfort between them. Clare broke the silence, 'if you don't mind me asking, what exactly happened?"

Tim chewed the inside of his mouth before answering. "She heard a conversation between me and Kris." Kris felt guilt waver through him like an ocean. Tim got up and made his way to the bar to pour himself a drink. Kris had basically called Robyn anti-social and weird whilst questioning Tim's choice in women.

His breathing became deeper at the way Clare's green eyes followed Tim's movements. He rubbed the base of his neck, noticing his fast-paced heartbeat.

"So, if the two of you were bitching about her, shouldn't *you* be the one apologising?" Tim made his way back to the sofa, avoiding Clare's darting gaze at him, "or, is there more to the story?"

Kris glanced at Tim, whose attention was on the glass in his hand. "Tim, what's Robyn's last name?"

"Wood." Kris rubbed his jaw, trying to think about all the names he had ever heard of. "You know the name?" Kris shrugged.

Clare opened her mouth to say something, "I think you should go home, Clare." Tim tilted his head up slightly from his glass.

Kris focused his gaze on Clare's piercing eyes. "Why? I'm not ten." He had never told her to leave his house before. His mind took in the two of them, sat so close to each other. A sickening emotion overtook him that combined with the heavy ball of string in his chest. The idea of them becoming a solid couple and Tim introducing Clare to his father pulled at the loose strings inside of him.

Kris gave her the excuse that it was getting late; it didn't seem to faze her, instead her head moved back, confused at his sudden turn of attitude. Clare raised her eyebrows at Tim, waiting for him to say something. Kris was quite surprised by Tim's lack of words as much as Clare was. She jumped off the sofa towards the cloakroom. Tim flinched at the sound of the front door slamming shut and placed his glass down before he stormed after her. Kris rolled his eyes; it seemed his idea backfired.

Kris made his way upstairs to get changed. When he came back down, Tim was sitting on the sofa staring into his empty glass. Kris slouched on the other end of the sofa and hung his head back.

"We're not together, you know." Kris didn't answer. He didn't want to have this conversation, or he would have to find an excuse to give Tim. "I don't want my ex to be wrapping wires around Clare's neck."

Kris angled his head towards Tim. "You haven't told Clare what Robyn did?" Tim shook his head. "But you told her that you and Robyn have broken up." Tim nodded. Kris faced his plain-white painted ceiling again. "How did she get home?"

Tim picked his glass up and went to the bar, "train." Clocks ticked for the next few minutes. Only the sound of Tim sipping his brandy could be heard. Neither of them said anything to each other. Kris then realised how hungry he was and that he'd left his plate in the living room. He didn't have the strength in him to go back and get it. The guilt of kicking his wife's sister out of his house sat on him like a large heavy portrait. "Do you ever plan on remarrying?"

Kris's insides quaked. He didn't know what was shown on his face, because Tim's gaze snapped back to his glass. Kris angled his head slightly so that he could see a picture of Kelci on top of the bar. She had hated taking pictures on her own. His mother managed to capture a picture of her on a day out together. Kelci was staring at the water, whilst her small hand kept the curls out of her face as they blew in the wind. "I had had feelings for Kelci for a really long time before we married." Kris said, avoiding Tim's gaze. "I think we should've spent more time together before rushing into marriage. I don't plan on remarrying any time soon. Maybe in the future, just not right now."

Tim removed his gaze from his glass. "Why did you ask her to marry so quickly?"

"At the time I didn't understand why Mum wanted me to marry so much. But I think it's because she knew she was dying, and she was scared I would always be alone." Kris felt his hands shake. He hadn't said that out loud. The words coming out of his mouth sent shivers up his arms.

"But you..." Tim glanced at Kris, "so you had liked Kelci for a really long time before you married?" Kris nodded. "Why didn't you just ask her out earlier?"

Kris felt the air go warm around him. He scuffed his hand through his hair before massaging his temple, "I was actually scared by how much I liked her." Kris had to look away from Tim when his eyebrows raised. "With other girls, I never used to like them that much, so I found it easy to just approach them. I could always speak to Kelci openly, but I used to close up every time..." Kris bit his tongue. "I remember one time in the car, I was trying to tell her that I didn't just like her. The words just wouldn't leave my mouth."

"Didn't Kelci catch on?" Kris smiled, shaking his head and remembering the way her face used to turn bright red. Tim grinned at him. "I didn't realise you were like that." Kris ran his hands over his face whilst dipping himself into the sofa. "So if you struggled with that, how the hell did you ask her to marry you?" Kris placed his head in his hands, "that bad?" Kelci flashed to the forefront of his mind. She stood with her small, round, squashed face in her sky-blue dress and her tiny hands in fists shouting at him in the middle of his restaurant. The very reason for their argument that day was the reason she had ended up saying yes to him. He explained to Tim how Kelci became angry without fully explaining why she was angry. Tim laughed, "when I proposed to her, I thought she was going to punch me in the face. I had to hold her arms down." Tim clutched his stomach in laughter.

They went silent for a few seconds. "What do you miss the most about her?"

Kris glanced at the clock and then brought his head down to his hands. He sensed her delicate, small hands in his and her pearl-green eyes peering straight into him. He saw the simplicity in her whilst staring at his hands, no eyeliner or coloured eyelids. She never wore it because she never needed it. In the distance he heard her ringing giggle. Then in the forefront of his mind he saw her lashes flutter and felt the soft tip of her miniature finger tracing his forehead. He beamed lightly, appreciating the realness of the moment.

Tim lifted himself up and a few seconds later Kris saw a glass being held out in front of him. "It's gone past dinner time." Kris rubbed his hands through his hair, unaware that Tim had picked up on his habits. "Do you think you could meet someone again?"

"I think Lauren has made many attempts at that." Tim showed a slight grin, "she's been making me meet every woman across London because she thinks I'm becoming lonely again," Kris rolled his eyes listening to Tim chuckle, "the last person…" Kris's eyes widened. "Estella Wood!"

Tim placed his drink on the table, "Lauren hooked you up with Robyn's sister?"

Kris tutted, "no! I went to meet one of Lauren's friends at a Chinese restaurant, the waitress's name was Estella Wood." Kris rubbed his jaw in thought whilst Tim rocked his head back on the sofa. "You're at work. I'll go there tomorrow at the same time I went last time, she's more likely to be there."

"What if they just happen to share the same last name?"

Kris shrugged his shoulders, "no harm in asking."

Tim nodded, "and then I can just move on with my life."

"What? With Clare?" Kris placed his drink down on the table, closing his eyes. He could feel the heat of Tim's stare on the side of his face. He twisted his head the other way, regretting the words that had left his mouth.

"You know," Kris forced himself to face Tim, who was now peering into his glass as he spoke, "I wouldn't do anything to piss you off." Kris nodded, knowing he wouldn't, because Tim was too much like his mother. She valued the people around her; his father didn't. "And I wouldn't do anything to hurt Clare." Kris gazed at him, seeing the truth as clear as day in his features. He wished his cousin knew.

~

Kris's eyes opened slowly. He had been tossing and turning and falling in and out of sleep for hours. He'd been thinking about the constant questions Tim had been asking him about Kelci. Her face kept swimming in and out of his mind like a wave and it kept knocking the air out of him every time she became clearer. He closed his eyes and shifted his body onto his side.

In the distance he heard her ringing giggle and his eyelids shot up. His heart jumped, seeing Kelci beside him. Kris knew this must be a dream, even though everything else around him was a haze, she was real. Her small mouth was smiling. His hands strained towards her, wanting to feel her fresh curls through his fingers. He couldn't move though. He suddenly felt the warmth of her small hands on his cheek as she shifted slightly closer to him and whispered, "stop looking back, Kris."

TUESDAY 17TH JANUARY 2012

Kris sat at his desk rubbing his temple. He was trying. He was trying really hard. Everyone around him always wondered why Kris spoke of his parents and Kelci so little. He did speak of them, just not much and it was because of moments like last night. They were there. Sitting in his thoughts as if they were jars on a shelf, half closed. As soon as they were mentioned, the jars would completely open again and it took too much of him to close them. He missed his parents and the ache of wanting his wife back in his life numbed him.

Though every part of him wanted to blame Jack for the loss of his family, the reality was that Jack was only the variable in what had happened to him. Kris's actions were his own. It was a stain that stuck to him no matter how much he tried to stick to Kelci's promise of living happily.

As Lauren walked in, Kris took in the time and then got up. Lauren began searching through a stack of papers on his desk. It then dawned on him that she had hardly said anything all day since he'd got in. "You alright?" She nodded, focused on flipping through the papers individually.

He lifted the collar of his jacket with his eyes narrowing, "Lauren?"

She lifted her eyes from the documents. "I'm fine, Kris." He squinted. 'Fine' wasn't a usual word in Lauren's dictionary. He decided to take his aunt's advice; she'd come to him if there was problem.

~

Kris sat at a red light with his window down. The nippy breeze that washed over him pinched away at the weight in his head. He tried not to close his eyes. The traffic light had been red for a surprisingly long time. He was third in line and the continuous way in which the car in front of him kept inching forward mirrored his impatience.

Kris began clicking his tongue and tapping his fingers on the dashboard. He instantly stopped, surprised by who he saw. He coughed lightly, wondering if he should beep. London drivers were already edgy, he didn't want to aggravate them by beeping in an intolerant queue, but he couldn't help himself.

She didn't turn when he pressed his horn. His Mercedes was usually quite loud. He eyed the traffic light. What was going on? How was it still red? His foot jumped off the brake a little when a tap on the passenger window startled him. He slammed his right foot back down on the brake before winding down the window. "Was that you beeping?" Her voice was light, reminding him slightly of a floating balloon.

He nodded, "where are you going? I can give you a lift?" She ran her long fingers through the tips of her hair, focusing her puzzled gaze at the pavement ahead of her. He glimpsed the traffic light, knowing it was about to turn amber, "I'm not going to attack you Adara, just get in the car and tell me where you need to go." She hastily got into the passenger seat with a pout. Just the way he expected, the traffic lights suddenly went amber, then green. He finally hit the gas with his head shaking. They made their way past Kensington Square gardens. "Where are we going?"

"The supermarket: all the way down, then left. I normally have my car, but it's gone in for service. I don't know how long it's going to take. And I took a today off, so I thought I'd go get some food since we're running out." Adara placed her bag down near her feet and Kris squinted, noticing the heels on her feet. He nodded before bringing his eyes back to the busy road ahead of them.

She unbuttoned her beige coat and made herself more comfortable in the seat.

"How's Reva?" Kris asked.

"She's okay." She glanced at him, "she keeps going on about that girl called Lauren."

Kris smiled, "she works in the office." He noticed the people moving in and out of the gaps between the parked cars. "How old is Reva?"

"She's twelve." Kris saw her turn to look at him out of the side of his eye. "Do you have any kids?" He felt his foot shake on the brake. He raised his eyebrows and moved his head side to side. "Sorry, because you're married and good with Reva, I assumed you would have had kids of your own." Kris took a quick glance at her eyes, gazing at him. He had no recollection of telling her or Reva he was married, so had no idea what his face was indicating. "You're wearing a wedding ring," Adara said.

He glimpsed the white gold satin band on his left hand and exhaled. He concentrated back on the road filled with people that were taking advantage of their hours' break from work. He cleared his throat, "she passed away a couple of years back." Adara stared at the pedestrians. "You?"

"Just me and Reva." Kris expected her to continue, instead she just gazed out of the passenger window. Kris rotated the wheel a tad, about to stop near three supermarkets he saw. 'Left there," Adara directed him.

Kris changed his direction, veering left. "How long are you going to be shopping? I could give you a lift back once I'm done with what I need to do." She shook her head, about to respond but he cut in, "so you're good with walking back with a load of heavy bags and those really uncomfortable looking shoes?" Kris placed his hand inside his jacket pocket.

He felt her scathing expression aimed at him, which made him grin. He parked up outside the supermarket. "I'll get a taxi."

He handed her his card, "well, if you change your mind and you prefer a free lift..." She placed the card in her bag and thanked him before leaving the car. "Try not to trip up!" He grinned. She turned and her pursed lips made his insides spin.

As she made her way inside, it dawned on him that he had no

idea which way it was to go back to the restaurant. Even so, he appreciated the longer drive. The roads were now not too packed, and he was thankful for the open street to drive freely on for half hour before he finally found the restaurant.

The mellow harp music was humming again softly in the background, creating an airy atmosphere along with the aromatic scents of cooking as Kris made his way through. He approached a short waiter, who appeared to be bored of his job, and asked for Estella. The waiter was polite enough to go find her while Kris waited by the entrance. The stringed instrument played on and he felt each pluck of a string pick at his brain as he stood patiently. He spun round when he felt a tap on his shoulder. Estella's large brown eyes beamed back at him with her high ponytail swinging behind her. "Hi, you called for me?"

Kris's brown eyes widened, realising how much of an awkward conversation this could turn into. "Yeah, I did. My name is Kris Dauni, we met the other week." She tilted her head slightly. Her eyes opened wide and her lips lifted slightly. He felt his face go bright red and she laughed. He rubbed his head, "it's Estella Wood, right?" She nodded her head slowly before flicking her massive eyes towards the customers. Kris rubbed the back of his head, wondering what was going through her mind. "Okay, erm… I don't know how to bring this up." Estella pointed at the restaurant, about to open her mouth. "–do you have a sister?"

Estella's soft expression snapped, and her posture stilled. "Robyn." Estella cut off Kris from continuing to talk, "look, she's my half-sister." She took a deep breath, "and I went through so much shit trying to contact her, and she ignored me like I was nothing to her. There's only so many slaps a person can take and now I'm done with her attitude. Now, sending some stranger to me…"

Kris raised his hands to stop her, "she doesn't know I'm here." Estella rolled her eyes. "Listen, I'm not here to listen to your whole family tiff, but she desperately needs support around her right now. Go see her." Estella looked at his hand, which was holding the paper with Robyn's address. "Please at least try, just one more time."

Thursday 1ˢᵗ March 1994

Adara was beginning to become used to her surroundings and the faces that visited the room they had left her in. They were mostly men. It seemed as if they just wanted something from her: she just didn't know what. She wished she knew. That way she could leave already. The view from her window seemed like a different world altogether and the prospect of running seemed frightening. She knew she had to stand up for herself. She took a deep breath and pulled herself from the bed. She had no clue what the time was, and there was no clock in the room.

She stroked her black hair out of her face with her shaking hands. She needed to show that she wasn't going to just quietly lay here like a rug to walk all over, otherwise she didn't know what they would do to her. She took a deep breath and stared at the door that was used most. The other door was a mystery to her, and if this didn't work, then that was her next target.

Taking another deep breath, she shoved her black hair out of her face again and pushed her legs forward. She hoisted her palms against the smooth, cream door. Her palms began to burn, "you can't leave me in here!"

She heard laughing and this shot a fire through her body, raising her screams. A few seconds later, she heard the handle click and she sprang her legs back. Her small feet were heaved up in a stance with her hands ready to knock out whoever entered. Her heels dropped when she saw who it was.

He raised his eyebrows at her. For some reason, she could easily shout and scream at the other men, this man however, seemed to have a certain quality in him that caught her breath. A tranquil youthfulness that radiated burden and strength; she didn't have the heart to be cruel to him.

"We did say that wouldn't help." He said, shutting the door behind him.

Adara puffed, aiming for the door. He caught her hand, pushing her back lightly, "Adara, the others won't be so polite." He stepped directly in front of the door, "play nice, please. Don't piss them off, and you will be out of here soon."

She cocked her head back, "and I just believe you."

He rubbed his head and Adara could feel the strain of the situation falling on his shoulders, "I get this isn't…"

She stepped forward, moving her shoulders back with fear tingling at the depths of her stomach. "You people have kidnapped me!"

Erikh shot his eyes at her, taking in the air around him. Adara's stared at him before her shoulders dropped with the understanding that he wasn't happy about this situation either. He swept his curtained hair back while she rubbed her eyes, removing any sign of tears from her face.

"At least tell me why I'm here. None of this makes any sense. I've never seen any of you." He removed something from his pocket.

"Just please co-operate and hopefully this will be over with quickly," he put his hand out and she saw a packet of the cola bottle sweets that she liked. Her eyebrows lifted at him and he threw the packet on the dressing table, "try to pass the time with some television or something. Dinner soon. I'll be back. Call me if you need anything and *please* play nice. I can't help you if you piss someone off."

He left the room, leaving Adara with her mouth open, confused by the encounter.

TUESDAY 17TH JANUARY 2012

Kris walked back to his office to find Lauren sitting at his desk. He halted at his door with his eyes widening, he checked behind him, seeing the empty reception. She smiled at him weakly. "It's my lunch." His eyes travelled to his clock. "Late lunch."

Kris exhaled, stepping further into the office before quietly closing the door behind him. He approached his desk: "I'm going to ask you one more time," he placed his hands on the desk, leaning in, "are you okay?"

She nodded whilst placing a ripped piece of lettuce in her mouth. Kris dropped his head, rubbing his temple. "My mum came to see me."

Kris controlled his display of happiness, "Lauren that's a good thing!" She peered down at the salad pot on the desk. "What's your view on it all?"

"I don't have one. I don't think so anyway. I don't know how she found me." She stared at the food in front of her, "she came. I let her in. She apologised. She left." Lauren was painted with defeat as her round eyes remained on the salad.

No matter how angry he was with his father for his blindness and pride, Kris would have had him alive in his life in a heartbeat. Kris swallowed, "Lauren, you want your mother back in your life. Otherwise, you wouldn't be thinking about it so much. She's apologised, which means she's accepted her mistake." Lauren blinked down at the desk. "When you're ready, give your mother a call." Kris felt his phone vibrate. He removed it from his jacket and beamed at the digits on the screen.

"Toodles." Kris lifted his eyes to see Lauren smiling lightly at him.

∼

Kris felt a surge of gratitude towards Adara's brother, who had taken their mother to Bath at the last minute. So now, Adara had to rush to pick up Reva from school. Adara placed her jacket on her lap whilst he drove through the traffic. He glanced back at her and noticed a black stone ring hanging from her neck on a thin, sliver chain. It wasn't a wedding ring and it wasn't a woman's ring either.

Adara looked at him the moment he brought his attention back to the road. "Kris, I haven't told you the directions to my house."

"It's five minutes till the school opens. What are you going to do? Go back home, take out all the shopping then be back within five minutes to pick her up?"

Adara chewed the inside of her lip whilst she stared out of the passenger window, "how do you know where her school is anyway?"

"Well there is only one school close by. She can't have travelled that far." Adara gazed back out the window. They stayed silent for a while, listening to the hustle and bustle of the streets and pedestrians around them. "Am I going the right way?" She nodded.

"Thank you." Adara said lightly whilst staring out of the passenger window. "Do you enjoy your job now?"

Kris's eyebrows pulled together with a sheepish smile, "now?"

She nodded. "I've always enjoyed my job and I still do, if that's what you're asking."

She nodded her head up and down slowly. A river of small children was flooding down the street, showing him that he was close to the school. "Reva asked me a question like that." Her dark-red, thick-lipped smile made his insides flutter. He parked outside the school gates watching all the children rushing past and reminding him of the school days that he had never missed.

After a few minutes, Reva jumped in the back of Kris's car, shouting his name in excitement. Kris hadn't been around children that much in his life other than the ones that attended Sani's play area; so, it surprised him how much Reva could talk. Within in a few minutes he learned that Reva found school boring and that she had another lazy lesson because of an absent maths teacher. His ears were also kept occupied by her lecture of her hatred for science, between Adara's directions to their house. She took them through the packed roads and grand houses.

"I never understand what the teacher is saying!"

Adara rotated in her seat to face her daughter, "so then why don't you ask?"

Kris noticed Reva drop her head slightly, though his attention remained on the roads ahead of him, "because everyone stares at me when I ask." Reva complained.

Kris wrinkled his eyebrows, "so what if they stare at you?" Reva drew back into the car seat, "you're never going to understand Reva, if you don't ask. Don't worry about the other children."

Adara nodded, "he's right. There is no shame in asking if you don't understand something."

Kris glanced at Reva from his car mirror. She was staring out of the window, avoiding her mother's attention with the string of her bag fiddling in between her fingers throughout the rest of the journey.

Kris was surprised by their house. It was neither small nor large. It was painted a brown colour, closer to red. The house had front gates, which he noticed Adara had opened from a fob attached to her keys. Both Reva and Adara jumped out the moment his car stopped in their driveway. Kris helped them take the bags out and placed them inside the hallway, which smelt of rosemary scented candles. He observed a large picture of Reva when she was younger and knew that this was around the time he had first met her at the hotel. Her hair was longer, and her cheeks were a little rounder: in the picture, Adara held onto her, giggling.

The house had a certain newness to it from the way the staircase's cream carpet was still fluffed and the walls seemed untouched.

As Kris placed the last of the bags on the hallway floor, Adara came towards him, biting her lips slightly. "Are you busy?"

Kris's owlish eyes held onto her fluttering gaze, which tried to dart away to the small bag of pasta in her hand, "what, now?" He asked. She nodded. "I guess not, why?"

He heard Reva sprint up the stairs the moment Adara chucked the bag of pasta into his hands, "you can continue helping then." Kris watched her make her way into the kitchen, surprised by her sudden invite.

Unknown of where the products went, he just helped with emptying the bags before Adara left him alone in the kitchen to refresh herself. He felt awkward, realising he was in someone else's house. He rubbed the back of his neck whilst taking in the cottagey-themed kitchen, which seemed to have a certain freshness to it. A few minutes later, Adara came down wearing a black hoodie and joggers. She made them both a coffee, and a hot chocolate for Reva.

Kris made his way into the living room to see Reva sitting in her blue pyjamas at the long, oak table doing her homework. The living room was simple and tidy. A flat screen television hung on the wall over a small fireplace and opposite was a long, brown leather sofa. There were pictures of Reva all over the room, consisting only from the time Kris had first met her. Some of the pictures had another, older lady, who Kris assumed was Adara's mother, and two other men. "My mum and brothers." Kris didn't realise Adara was standing next to him, clutching onto the ring around her neck. Her hair was effortlessly tied up and the angles in her face had suddenly been defined. With her make up removed, her features seemed so much more revived. "My older brother lives outside London and my other brother lives a few roads down from me with his wife. My mum lives in her own flat. I'm the youngest." Kris nodded, while taking a quick glance over at Reva, who had her head stuck in her books. "I'm quite close with my younger brother." She pointed at a picture on the wall which showed Reva smiling with her uncle, again the picture was recent. Probably a little while after Kris had first met her. "But he can be a complete idiot sometimes. His wife thinks so too." Kris sensed her staring at him from the side when he smiled. "What about you?" She asked.

Kris exhaled, thinking of the right words to use. "It's just me. Parents passed away a few years back and then after that my wife died in a car crash. I have my aunt and cousin." He felt like Adara's grey eyes were exploring his thoughts. He avoided her stare with heat flushing through his face.

"And your Dad?"

Adara shook her head like she'd just been woken up, "join me in the kitchen, I'm making spaghetti." Kris's head tilted to the side before following her and offering to help. She insisted he drink his coffee instead, "spaghetti is Reva's favourite. She likes it a specific way." Adara said smiling. She placed the spaghetti in the salted water and then put the pan on the hob before returning to the garlic. Kris grinned lightly, watching the spaghetti sitting in water.

"I haven't had spaghetti in ages. I'm more of a lasagne fan." Kris said. He lifted his eyes away from the spaghetti.

"Really? I thought you would've been more penne. It's served quite a bit at your restaurant." Kris tilted his neck, narrowing his eyes at her. She teased, "I don't know if you keep updated with your records, but your restaurant is quite popular in London."

Kris glanced at the spaghetti before he watched her continuing to chop the garlic, "how come you invited me in?" Adara's eyes snapped up at him and squinted. He grinned, evaluating her confused features, "last time I saw you, you were ready to beat me."

She exhaled, returning her attention to the garlic, "that's a bit of an exaggeration." He bit the inside of his cheek, gazing at the gleaming floorboards, "normal adult company is refreshing." He glimpsed back at her, "makes a change from my over-critical mother and my ten-year-old man-child of a brother," she explained. Kris grinned. "–and you did confirm you wouldn't attack me."

Kris chuckled, watching her place the garlic in a pan. Reva came through the kitchen, stopping Adara from turning the gas on, complaining, "Mum I'm hungry!"

Adara eyed her daughter, "patience, Reva."

Reva crossed her arms, "why don't I order some pizza?" Kris grinned when Adara pouted. He pointed at the hob, making Reva lightly clap her hands in laughter. Kris slowly backed away from the counter, "sorry I wanted to tell you, but the longer you didn't realise the funnier I found it." Adara's eyes whizzed around at the hobs, "you haven't put the gas on for the spaghetti." They both listened to Reva's ringing laugh while Kris felt the breath knocked out of him from the way Adara's grey eyes pierced into him.

After a few minutes, Adara was eventually persuaded. Kris helped Reva complete her maths homework whilst waiting for the pizza to arrive. Reva was better at maths than she had let on; her dislike for science was a different story altogether. Once the pizza arrived and they had finished eating, Reva went to watch television, leaving Adara and him at the table. Kris stared at Reva from across the table before he glanced at Adara then back at Reva again. "You seem as if you want to say something?" Adara asked.

Kris rubbed the base of his neck, "you haven't said anything about Reva's father." The dimmed spark in her sharp grey eyes defeated the smile on her face. She fiddled with the ring around her neck again, with her eyes fixated on the table in front of her. She then bolted up and collected the dishes.

"He died abroad." Kris analysed the way her eyes focused on the dishes she was picking up. He offered to help her, but she replied brusquely, "no thanks, but help yourself to more wine if you want some."

Their conversations remained general until Adara's mood shifted back to normal. Eventually, he decided to leave, not wanting to overstay his welcome. Kris couldn't shake the feeling that there was a massive wall between them, and he just couldn't tell if either of them wanted to remove it or not.

Sunday 8th May 1994

Months had passed. She would cuddle further into her blankets whenever the weather dropped. Her last thought whenever she fell asleep was of her parents. She missed her parents. She missed her older brothers. She never thought that would happen, so on days like today it made her value her life so much more. She had lost the right to pick up the phone whenever she wanted. She had lost the right to walk out the door. She had lost the right to eat whenever her stomach asked for food. She had lost the right to shower or bath whenever she wanted. She had lost the right to change her clothes or brush her hair, whenever she needed. She wanted to know where she was. She would wake in the morning and just stay in bed. Where could she go? She was stuck in one hotel room. Every now and then someone would walk in to check that she was still there. She was thankful though, that that was all that they did.

Sometimes she wondered, how these people were renting the room out for so long? How was this all working? Did no one in the hotel notice anything suspicious? A group of people never leaving the room and never letting room service come through the door. It must seem odd to someone.

She could watch television if she wanted, but the stories or characters didn't appeal to her because all she wanted was to go home. She would wander around the room aimlessly, waiting for something to happen.

She would have visions of a policeman walking in randomly and explaining that everything had been sorted. These bad people were going to go to jail, and she could go back to her parents. Sometimes, she would imagine herself a princess being saved from her locked room by a man on a horse. She never thought there would come a day where she wanted to be a fairy tale character. Those stupid thoughts were what pulled her through the day.

She was sitting on the bed one day when Erikh walked through the door waving a sandwich. "Lucky me," she answered in a high-pitched voice while staring out of the window. She had concluded that if anything, these people weren't going to harm her. She tried to make sense of the whole situation. They had taken her, held her hostage, refused to harm her, so instead treated her like an animal? None of it added up. They needed something from her.

Adara now confirmed that Erikh was the decent one of the lot. There was a hidden sensitivity to him that struck her. He didn't appear the way the others did. Unlike the others, he seemed more on guard rather than aggressive. He hardly threatened her, just warned her. Not a harsh warning, more like the warning that a friend gives her best friend to be careful of the bad boy in the school.

Erikh always remembered to bring her food twice a day and sometimes with it he would sneak in magazines and books to read. He would tell her to hide them whenever the big one, Malum, entered the room. Apparently, Malum felt that books and magazines would give her ideas of ways to escape.

"Could the television not do that too?" Adara responded when Erik said this to her.

"Well don't say that to him, otherwise you'll deny yourself another privilege." Erikh rolled his eyes. He walked further into the room and approached her bed. "You know you're going to get hungry later, so I would just stop being stubborn and eat it." Her impulse to shout was interrupted by him chucking something in front of her on the bed. Her eyes sprung open at her favourite red lace sweets; she blinked at him in confusion before reaching out for them. "I know things." He instantly snatched them back.

He shot his small, dark eyes at the sandwich and she gritted her teeth. She picked it up and bit into it with a heavy sigh. She kept her eyes on Erikh whilst chewing into the cucumber and cheese. He stood rubbing his head. On his hand was a thick, silver, black stone ring. Everyone else wore rings and chains that they changed every day. Adara noticed that his ring hadn't left his finger. Erikh's attention was focused on the ground. He seemed like someone had beaten him with a heavy dumbbell without leaving any signs of bruises or scratches. "You look tired."

She noticed a silver chain on his neck that was different and thinner from the ones the others were wearing. He lifted his gaze from the ground to meet her eyes, "babysitting a grown child does that to you."

She shrugged, "you don't have to. I don't know why I'm here

anyway, you've not asked for money or anything." Erikh rolled his eyes and threw the sweets on the bed before walking out.

Tuesday 14th February 2012

The office had been quiet today and he knew it was because of the heavy snow slowing the London trains. Most of his employees had decided to work from home to avoid being stuck in the humid, claustrophobic trains for hours. It had been a few days since he'd seen Adara and Reva. The change of atmosphere from when he had asked about Reva's father wasn't what he'd expected. Wasn't it a basic question though? She had openly told him of the rest of her family, wasn't asking about the father expected? His thoughts assured him of one question. He'd had enough drama in his life to spot where a secret was hidden.

Kris did want to see them again, but there was so much in the way. It wasn't just the nagging questions on his mind, it was also that he hadn't apologised to Clare yet. He didn't know how to. In her perspective, there was no reason for the way he kicked her out, and even though there was, he still didn't like that he had to do it. The day Kris had been with Adara, he was slightly surprised that Tim hadn't called him to ask about Estella. To Kris, this meant that he was with Clare. Their growing closeness was turning into a relationship and that thought produced heavy ropes inside his chest that stifled his breathing.

Kris clicked the lid of his yellow highlighter up and down on the pen, trying to register the long-winded document he was reading. He hated the legal side of his work, it was the only aspect that he procrastinated from. He found all the regulations and conditions a very mundane procedure; nevertheless, it had to be done and he'd taken this day out to read it before handing it over to the legal team.

Kris lifted his head up to his open door. They'd been laughing on and off for the past few minutes. He assumed someone must've played a joke. He traced his eyes back to the document whilst continuing to click his highlighter. He heard an uproar of laughing again and his head snapped up. He rolled his eyes, readying himself to get up and close the door. He stopped when Reva came sprinting into his office and flung his arms around him. Kris's eyes sprung open and he pushed her back, staring at her dimples before she ran back out of his office. Kris rubbed his hand through his hair, not knowing whether to be happy about seeing Reva, or worried that Adara may be having a panic attack.

He picked up his phone and searched for her number, he texted:

It's Kris, Reva is at the office. She's fine. She's having fun with Lauren. Don't worry. Don't panic! She's safe.

Kris placed his phone back on his desk, wondering whether he should have rung her instead. He picked up his highlighter and began clicking the lid on and off again. He eyes whizzed across the paper at all the words that looked like a tornado of letters. His phone beeped and he picked it up:

Kris, I'm so sorry! I'm on my lunch. I can come and pick her up now.

Kris grinned, listening to his fingers tap against his phone:

I said she's safe Adara. Pick her up when you're done.

She wasn't lying when she said she was on lunch; her response came within seconds:

I finish work late. Hair appointment for 'Sweet Sixteen'.

Kris chewed the inside of his mouth before responding:

She enjoys spending time with Lauren, so pick her up from mine when you're done?

He saw the message was read and her response came after a few seconds:

Reva talks about her a lot. She's the one that was in the car with you, right?

Kris blinked at her message before replying:

I guess it's because Reva likes her. And yes, she was in the car. Do you not have greasy hair to get back to?

His message was instantly read. He waited a few seconds before putting his phone down and placed his eyes back on his tornado of regulations and conditions. He blinked at the paper, trying to bring the words into focus. He heard a load of laughter outside and wondered if anyone was actually working. He rolled his eyes before glancing out of the window behind him. London was filled with the last shards of winter. People's pace of breathing could be seen in the air and shops were filled with hats for protection from the snow that rose up to people's knees. Reva had managed to make it to his office in the heavy snow. He shook his head. That mother probably lost Reva whilst she was on an outing. Adara needed to find better friends to take care of Reva.

His phone beeped:

Lauren's your employee?

Kris rubbed the base of his neck before he began typing:

I thought we'd established that?

The message was immediately read. He rubbed his head before he began typing again and hitting send:

She's also a close friend. I've known her for years.

Her response came a within seconds after the tick became blue:

Yes, I do have greasy hair to get back to. And, just to let you know I love my job! Happy Valentine's day by the way. Thanks for taking care of Reva. See you soon!

Kris's eyes widened, staring at the message with his mouth agape. He hadn't fully acknowledged the date. He would've responded if she hadn't had ended the conversation. He placed his phone down on the table. He referred back to the document in front of him and then chucked the highlighter over it before swinging his head back. The laughter roared loud outside again.

∼

Tim felt like he was going to enter battle. He stood outside his old flat with Clare. He had to see Robyn to know she was okay. She was going through a rough period, he wanted to be there for her. There was only so much he could do, which is why he had brought Clare. He had to tell her. Clare had suffered from a similar state after the loss of her sister, so he knew Clare might be able to help Robyn more than he could. She had taken time off of work for this and he appreciated her dedication, however, it didn't change the heavy dread he was encountering. He was taking the girl that he was now completely into to meet his extremely high tempered ex! Life couldn't get any more complicated for him right now.

He stared at Clare. He knew he was completely falling for her, and he knew Clare liked him too. That was obvious. It scared him.

Not the emotion, the possible consequences. Tim had only just built his relationship with Kris. Did he really want to throw that out the window? Nevertheless, as a friend or cousin, wouldn't Kris just want them to be happy? Did Kris think that badly of him? He wouldn't hurt Clare. He couldn't imagine that but, if their relationship didn't work, then the repercussions with Kris involved didn't seem inviting: especially after his reaction to seeing them the other day. Kris's cold stare since then was scarred in his brain.

One issue at a time. Tim opened his door and shouted out for Robyn. The house was completely tidy. No small mirror in the living room and no fruit bowl. There was a tear in the middle of the sofa with no trace of the bits of cotton. Everything was back in its place. Clare came in behind him, hitting his arm.

Robyn sat at the small dining table. Her hair was neat, tied in a bun. Her features were drained and colourless. Her brown eyes were glassy. She didn't seem to acknowledge that someone had entered the flat.

Tim closed the door behind them and approached Robyn. Her eyes remained on the plate of hardened chips in front of her. Clare gingerly sat down next to Robyn. "We thought we'd come and see how you were." Tim placed his hands in his pockets. He'd been through this before and it was exhausting.

Clare swallowed and gazed at Robyn, "Robyn, what are you thinking about?" Robyn turned her head slowly to Clare, making Tim gulp. "Robyn, I may not be able to completely know what you're going through, but I can understand if you're overwhelmed."

Robyn's eyes narrowed. "Understand."

Clare exhaled, then tucked her hair behind her ear. Robyn blinked, "I've known you for a while now, you're my friend and I want you to know you're not alone."

Robyn's eyes bore into Clare and Tim wanted to grab Clare's arm and drag her out of the flat, away from Robyn. "You're not my friend. You just pity me. Has Tim been giving you updates on how much of a freak I am?

"You're not a freak Robyn." Robyn sprang from her chair and Tim grabbed hold of Clare's arm with the intention of taking her out of the flat. She tutted before shrugging his hand off. "Robyn, you're sick of everyone. Right?"

Robyn's hands flew to the sides of her head, "you don't understand."

Clare tilted down to look at her. "Then help me to understand, help me to understand what you're feeling Robyn. I promise that I genuinely care and so does Tim." Robyn bottled up and Clare followed behind her watching her hold onto the side of her head. The sound of a knock on the door did not seem to catch the women's attentions. Tim ignored it until the knock came harder. He stormed to the door, ready to turn whoever it was away.

In front of him stood a tall, brown-eyed woman with a really high ponytail. "I don't know if I got the right place," she glanced at the door number, "I was told Robyn Wood lives here?" His mouth dropped.

∼

Robyn's ears were lying. It wasn't her sister's voice that she was recognising. She found her ears hadn't deceived her, because her shield completely shattered when her little sister appeared in front of her. She had spent years building her armour, and within seconds her sister had the power to make them completely crumble. A chill swept through the air that vibrated through her small body. She felt inferior and dirty in front of her perfectly-dressed sibling. She was wearing a long, red blouse underneath her blue jacket and her black knee-high boots seemed to compliment her strangely matched ensemble.

Robyn instinctively stepped back when Estella moved closer. Clare and Tim watched her refusing to meet her sister's eyes, who for some reason had begun crying. "Robyn, please talk to me."

Those words snapped a wire in her head, making her scream. It was too late when Clare noticed her hand stretch towards a knife in the sink. The knife flew in the air and Tim quickly shoved Estella out of harm's way with a swift movement of his arm. Robyn's eyes widened at the space at which the knife had just flown. She knew she'd just thrown a knife across the room, but the act felt more like a nightmare rather than something real. Shame seeped into her skin, bringing in nausea with it. Her legs ached. The heaviness of them brought her knees down to hit the ground. "Please just leave me alone."

"Can I please have some time alone with my sister?" Estella asked. Robyn closed her eyes, shaking her head in refusal. She heard the door slam after feeling a faint stroke on the side of her ear. The words, "it's okay," rang lightly in the air and she shivered. The voice was familiar, and it wasn't Estella's. She shuddered while hearing the noise of Estella's boots approach her. She instantly shoved her back against the cupboard and brought her knees in. She saw Estella sit down in front of her on the floor. She refused to look at her face. "We're not sixteen anymore, Robyn." Robyn placed her chin on her knees, staring at the leg of the chair in front of her, "think of all the time we've wasted not talking." She rolled her eyes, turning her face the other way. "I thought you would've at least asked how Mum is."

Robyn resisted the urge to tear at her sister's skin by interlocking her fingers, "the witch not dead yet?"

There were a few seconds of silence. "Yeah, she is." Robyn felt a rock fling through the pit of her stomach. Her mouth went dry and her chest twisted from the feel of a dagger tearing into it. Estella's face was wet with tears, "I argued so much with Mum after you left. You may not have been her daughter, but she had no right to kick you out of our father's house. At eighteen, I went to live with one of my friends. I tried contacting you and I eventually went back to Mum. When I went back…" More tears ran down Estella's face. "She was gone."

Robyn stared at her sister with the pain of a dagger digging deeper into the middle of her chest, "I may not have been her daughter?"

Estella blinked.

Robyn pointed at her, "you're hers, but I'm not." Robyn scanned the room, trying to find a way to tie together the loose threads in her mind. Her hands clutched at the sides of her temple. "I don't understand, I'm older than you."

Estella sniffed and breathed deeply. "When Mum and Dad got married, he didn't tell her that he'd been married before and that he'd already had a child. Your mother walked out on you before she died. A few days after they married, Dad told Mum. You can imagine, Mum was so embarrassed, which is why she stayed in the marriage. Then Dad died a few months after I was born. Mum couldn't leave you on your own, so she brought you up with me."

Robyn closed her eyes, "that doesn't make any sense Estella, how can Dad have me on one side and then another family on the other?"

"Robyn, I don't know the full story, I'm sure there's so much more, but that's all Mum told me on the night she kicked you out."

Estella flinched and shrugged her sister's small hand off her arm, muttering, "leave." Estella's wet lashes fluttered at her. "You need to go. On top of the way she treated me, you treated me just as badly." Estella's eyes widened at her sister, her mouth open, wanting to say something. Robyn hauled herself up from the floor with the weight of the bricks rolling around inside of her. She pointed her finger at the door with her teeth grinding. Estella's face burnt red with tears. "I said, leave!"

Robyn didn't watch her sister; she dropped back to the floor after hearing the door slam shut. She laid her head down on the cool marble floor, letting it cool her burning head. So many questions. Endless questions. She curled her body into herself like a foetus and allowed her heavy eyelids to drop. The mother's arms that she had craved so long to cradle her weren't even the arms of her biological mother. If her biological mother didn't even want her, why would any woman want her?

Before this situation, she had a family that hated her. Now, she didn't even belong to a family. Before, she had an unfulfilling father and a mother that despised her. Now, she had no parents and her half-sister made her feel small and worthless.

She took a deep breath. Her chest burnt and ached with heaviness. She felt her head move in circles, whilst her tears dripped fast down her warm cheeks and formed a small puddle on the marble beneath her. She tried to control her hyperventilated breathing. Her eyes saw complete blackness, even though her mind was racing with pictures of her mother's sharp and spiteful expression.

She took in the air around her through her nose and then suddenly felt a chill rush past her body that made her huddle in further. Her misty eyes sparked open from the chilly sensation that swept over her forehead. Her head remained on the floor and she was about to jolt up until she heard a light shushing whisper in her ear that slowed down her breathing. She closed her eyes again.

After a few hours Robyn picked herself up and locked the door. She walked to the dining table. Chips and broken glass lay on the carpet. She had no intention of cleaning the mess up. A piece of paper caught her attention.

If you ever change your mind. I'm here for you.
07905068976
Your sister always,
Estella.

Friday 26th June 1994

Adara heard the door open behind her and she retreated further into the bedsheets that she felt kept her safe. It was only when she heard him call her name in that guarded voice that she popped her head out curiously. He never came into her room at this time. His aura resonated protection, although she knew she should be scared. She pulled herself up on the bed. She furrowed her thick eyebrows at Erikh questioningly at the way he stepped further into the room. Surprisingly, he cracked a contagious smile.

"So, I was wondering if you wanted a break from this room?" She shot out of the bed like a kangaroo immediately, "–but!" He indicated a blindfold in his hand, "I'm going to have to cover your eyes until we leave the place."

She dropped her stiff shoulders, "how are you going to get me out of here anyway? Aren't there a bunch of idiots ready to laugh outside the door?"

Erikh's thick lips lifted into a smile again, "no, they've all decided to go and take a long break and I've been left to babysit you." She bit the inside of her mouth, "so, would you like to stay in here or would you like some fresh air?"

"Why do I have to be blindfolded?"

He waved the black blindfold, "so you can't figure out where we are." She pursed her lips at the way his arm lingered between them. "Yes or no?" She bit her lip. She couldn't help feel this aura of trust radiating from him and she wanted to leave the room. Even if it was only for a little while. "and don't think of playing any stupid tricks, Adara. Otherwise, you'll only create more trouble for yourself."

Her sharp grey eyes lingered on him and she bit her lip slightly, "why are you doing this? Wouldn't you get in trouble?"

He went quiet, dropping his arm back down, "so you want to stay here?" She stepped closer to him, instantly closing her eyes ready to be blindfolded. He strolled behind her and wrapped the blindfold over her eyes slowly. She gulped hesitantly. "You're fine. Don't worry," he soothed. She felt her chest relax and her shoulders drop.

Before she knew it, his heavy hands were on her shoulders, slowly guiding her. Her breathing staggered at the unrecognisable breeze that brushed against her cheeks. There was bustling in the background that made her head turn. Her chest went up and down in motion with her slightly chaotic breathing. She placed her hands on the blindfold, then immediately felt his hand clasp her wrist, "not yet."

The walk lasted a few long minutes, and she could feel her insides jumping with anticipation. Her foot dipped and she wobbled, "sorry, should've told you about that." The ground suddenly felt soft in comparison to the hard-levelled floor before. Humidity overtook her senses and she inhaled deeply the mugginess around her.

A few seconds passed and her eyes fluttered open to rows of greenery. High trees and a dark sky filled her sights. She swivelled her eyes to Erikh and he waited for her to say something.

"It's a field." She tilted her head questioningly, "there isn't anything here."

He gave a throaty laugh and shrugged his shoulders, "just fresh air."

He placed himself down on ground, tapping the grass in front of him. She blinked. He brought her out to an empty field. There was nothing, just nature surrounding them. She didn't know what she was expecting. The non-existence of buildings hadn't occurred to her at all though. She couldn't even see the building that could possibly be holding her hostage. He made sure to keep their location completely hidden.

"Not to your standards?" She glanced at him, "at least be thankful that you have some fresh air. I know I am." She stared at him, realising how trapped he was.

She breathed deeply and observed the sky above her. The warm air rushed through her nose and a freeing sensation took over her.

Although nature was never something that attracted her, today it seemed to give her a hope that she hadn't felt in a long time. It made her feel like she'd been brought to life again. Time had a new meaning now; standing around life itself reminded her of what it felt like to live. "Why did you bring me out?"

He rolled his eyes, pulling at the grass, "would you have preferred to stay in that room?"

"But you could have left me inside." She sat down next to him. Erikh kept his eyes focused on the grass he was ripping at and she stared at him. Knowing that Erikh was around told her that she could get through this: "thank you." Erikh shrugged his shoulders.

They went silent for a little while, listening to the night that took over her being completely. She hadn't felt this calm in such a long time. She looked at Erikh again, whose sight was still focused on the grass.

"What would happen if someone found out you took me out of the room?"

He froze. His sharp eyes turned to her, "why? Is someone going to find out?"

She shook her head quickly, indicating no. He rolled his eyes with a sigh and tore at the grass again, "tell me a little about them," she implored.

"There isn't anything to tell, but I can tell you who not to piss off."

TUESDAY 14TH FEBRUARY 2012

He had managed to highlight some parts of the document that needed to be inspected by the legal team for the building that he was buying from Gal. It was a long process that he'd managed to get halfway through. His phone beeped and he glanced at it. It was Adara asking him for his home address. He checked the time and rubbed his head with guilt flooding through him. He replied, telling her they were still in the office. It was just Reva, Lauren and himself left behind after a long day.

He called for Lauren, swiping his card from his wallet. Reva hung behind Lauren, who was wearing a sky-blue furry jumper with multi-coloured butterflies. Kris blinked his eyes; the jumper had too much going on for his brain to take in. Lauren flashed her teeth, making him rub his aching head.

Reva dropped on the chair and placed her small face in her hand. He was sure having a kid in the office was child labour in some way. He handed his card to Lauren with his eyes set on Reva, "your choice of food."

She sprang her face up with a broad grin, "pizza and rainbow cake!"

Kris chuckled to himself lightly. Lauren grinned, taking the card, "and a bottle of red." His lips fell. She shrugged, "hey she chooses the food and I choose the drink."

Reva jumped off her chair, shrugging her shoulders, "it's only fair!" Kris's owlish eyes narrowed in on Reva. She dropped her arms with her doe-eyes widening, "I get tropical juice of course." He heard Lauren giggling before they made their way out the office. He let out a sigh and began clearing his desk. After ten minutes of packing everything away in his briefcase, he locked his office door and ignored his vibrating mobile. He rushed down to reception. His throat went dry from seeing her after such a long time. Her long fingers dropped her phone into her brown bag, which matched her long, beige coat. She was less tall than he remembered and realised she had switched her heels for flats. Her widened grey eyes whizzed around him. "Reva's gone with Lauren for pizza. They won't be long."

She leaned against the reception counter and twisted her neck. "Don't your office lot get annoyed with her when they're trying to work?"

Kris clicked his tongue, "she brightens the atmosphere up a bit, and she likes handing things over to different teams." He leaned against the reception sofa. "I'm sure there's something against that though."

Adara nodded with her thick lips turning into a smile, "I'm sure too. I should file a lawsuit. Child labour."

Kris grinned at his hands. "How was the greasy hair?"

She rolled her eyes, "please don't." Her hands soothed the back of her neck, making Kris chuckle. "sixteen-year olds drive me mental. I don't understand how parents can let their child become so spoilt. If you can't handle them, then don't have them."

Kris glanced at her raising his eyebrows. "That's a bit of bold statement. Some parents just want children no matter how hard it is. You can't judge every parent based on their child."

Adara stood up straight and placed her hands in her pockets. "They're the ones bringing the child up."

Kris shifted his head back whilst she stared at him. "Yeah, but the parents can't be in the child's life twenty-four seven. A parent can influence a child's thinking, but not control the way their child behaves particularly. School, friends and whatnot begin to influence them too throughout their teens."

Adara blinked at him and then stormed out of the reception. Kris stood still for a second in dismay at her sudden reaction, before he followed her to the car park. She spun around, forcing him to step back, "it's the parent's responsibility to teach them right from wrong!"

Kris searched her angular face, trying to find the root of her thinking. Her dark eyes blended into the night. He breathed, taking in the rosemary-scented candles from her coat, "and over time a child creates their own ideas of right and wrong," he said.

She gritted her teeth before turning and backing away from him, her thick hair whipping into his face. His mouth hung agape watching Adara storm to her car, slamming the door shut. He heard the sound of his car, telling him that Lauren had arrived back. Reva approached him gleefully with a bag of pick'n'mix sweets swinging from her arm. He tried to smile at her, but his attention was on Adara's stare, which was fixed on the steering wheel of her car.

Adara let out a sigh and unclenched her jaw at the sight of her daughter. "Reva, get in the car please." Reva's eyes zoomed from Kris to the pizza. Lauren looked at him, then at Adara pulling at her sleeves. Kris then rubbed his forehead, before taking out the pizza and banging the passenger door shut. Reva flinched at the sound and watched, confused at the scene unfolding in front of her whilst her mother repeated for her to get into the car. Kris made his way to Adara's Volkwagen Golf and placed the pizza in the back seat. He steadied his breathing to tap on the driver's seat window. Reva quietly approached the passenger seat, gaping at her mother, who eventually rolled her eyes before bringing down the window.

He bent his knees down so he was level with Adara, who had a stiff stare fixed at her wheel, "I'm sorry if I offended you in some way, and happy valentine's day to you too," he said. She glanced down at her fidgeting hands before motioning to Reva to get into the car again. Kris sighed and peered over the car, "I'll see you soon Reva." Reva squinted her eyes and ran up to him with a hug. "I promise." She nodded before letting go and jumping into the passenger seat. Kris jumped back from the car as it flew out of the car park.

Lauren had moved to the passenger seat before Kris arrived back at his own car. He got in and switched on the ignition. She bit her lip with impatience.

"She's bloody crazy. One minute she's talking perfectly fine then the next she's going off on one!" he exclaimed. Lauren began laughing. "It's not funny! I don't know what the hell to do!" Kris was thankful that he didn't have to hit the brake. The roads were empty because of how late it was, which meant he was able to take his frustration out on his gas pedal.

Lauren put her head down, suppressing her laugh. "What was the argument about?"

"It wasn't even an argument! I don't know even know what the hell that was!" Kris rubbed his head before explaining her sudden outburst and Lauren giggled. "What? What did I say? Was the fact that I voiced my own opinion not right? Is this some new rule that I don't know about? Where a man can't have an opinion when the woman is having a bad day?" Memories of some of the arguments he had with Kelci flooded back to him. At least she'd eventually snap and tell him what was going on in her brain, or else Kris would just know what she was angry about. He rolled down his window, breathing in the wintry London air, which broke down the anger bottled in his chest.

Lauren giggled, "Kris, all this time she's probably been thinking that she can govern how Reva turns out. Now you've just gone and laid it on her that there are other things that could influence Reva that aren't in her control. She's probably just feeling pressured."

Kris rubbed his head while he pressed harder on the gas, "so then why didn't she just say that!?" He hit his steering wheel, "get Tim on the phone. He called me earlier." He exhaled again, wondering what on earth he had got himself into. The cause of this whole argument was that stupid big wall Adara had placed between them and he was beginning to get sick of it. Even if he wasn't completely ready to move it, he was willing to try and take the first step. He couldn't do that though, if she was continuously increasing the size of the wall. Though he and Kelci hardly ever spoke during the last years of their marriage, at the beginning he never had this problem. Then again, most of the time it was Kelci taking the weight of their marriage on her shoulders. He suddenly felt a rush of guilt from being on the other side of the table. He exhaled, and then felt Lauren squeeze his shoulder.

Lauren pressed the call button on his car system, and they began listening to the ring resonating from the speakers.

The ringing stopped and Lauren shouted, "Tim, I've got Kris in the car with me!" The voice that came back greeting them wasn't Tim's. Lauren bit the inside of her mouth, watching Kris clench his jaw at the road ahead of him. Kris pulled in the breeze from his window and took a deep breath. Lauren gulped, "ermmm Kris said he had a missed call from you."

"Yeah, I just wanted to say thanks. Estella came." Tim said as Kris nodded his head noting how Clare had gone silent, "I'm going to drop Clare home and I'll see you in a bit." He turned into a long silent side road that was lined with houses and flats that were mostly owned by Dauni's Estates.

Lauren put the phone down, "did you apologise to Clare?" Kris had told Lauren about how he had kicked Clare out his house. He chose to remain quiet rather than bear the shame of his inactions. "The longer you leave it, the more upset she's going to be." Kris chewed the inside of his mouth. "Look, Tim and Clare are grown adults and Clare isn't stupid. She doesn't even like Tim's father." Kris raised his eyebrows at her, "we do talk about you and Tim you know." Kris rolled his eyes. Lauren smiled and placed her hand on his shoulder, "don't worry, not *everything* we say is horrible about you." He ignored her to focus on the way he parked outside Lauren's flat. "She's a big girl, Kris. She'll tell you if anything's wrong, but you need to apologise to her." Kris gazed out of the window and sighed before nodding. "As for Adara…" Kris watched her talk down to her hands, "personally I would struggle to tell people that I'm scared about raising my child alone." Lauren hastily waved her hands to prevent him from arguing, "the point is though, that you like her, so if you want to form a relationship with her, you need to try a little harder."

Kris exhaled, "what if there isn't supposed to be a relationship?" He squinted out of the window, biting his lip before his eyes travelled down to his left hand. With Kelci, everything was completely natural. His whole relationship just fell into place with her; he never had to try and make things work. It just happened.

"Kris." He looked at Lauren, "…it's been a little while. You're not even a couple or anything and you're already stressing. Just give her some time to open up to you. You technically haven't known her that long. Maybe you'll realise that you don't actually like her that way and that you'd prefer her to be more of a friend in your life, but right now you like her, so try to find out if there is actually something there."

They went quiet for a little while, concentrating on the road, before Kris broke the silence. "Have you called your mother yet?"

SATURDAY 20TH AUGUST 1994

For a random change and just for the sake of doing something different during the day, Adara dragged the sheets off the mattress and made herself a little bed on the floor. No one could say anything to her. It wasn't like she was trying to escape. The other day, she had become so increasingly frustrated that she had attempted the front door – the unused, mysterious door. She hadn't even reached it when Erikh had walked in, dragging her back, "it's not worth it." He pushed her back to the bed, "you're just going to end up getting yourself in trouble."

For the past couple of weeks, Adara noticed Erikh appearing

more drained than usual. She resisted questioning him about why he was looking so exhausted in the fear that he would get annoyed. If anything, Adara was more upset about the fact that she was denied information. She wanted to know where she was, what was behind the main door, why these people wanted to keep her here and if her parents had even started searching for her. She had loss count of how many days it had been. She couldn't imagine what her family were going through. The thought ripped into her. She wanted to tell her mother she was still alive, and that if there was any goodness left in the world, then she'd be home soon, and she'd never leave to go out to late night showings again.

"What's happening here? Thought you'd jazz the place up?" Adara ignored the tall woman, she didn't need to see who it was to know who it was. She could recognise Vidia's distinct accent from anywhere. Erikh had warned her that no matter how nice Vidia tried to act, the string of her spikes weren't to be tested. Vidia was Malum's weakness and strength in so many ways. You break one of Vidia's spikes and Malum would feed you to her for lunch. Whenever Vidia entered her room, Adara accepted Erikh's word and kept her head down. She wanted to keep hold of the hope of leaving this place. The only way to do that would be to stay in everyone's good books and try to get some information from someone about why she was there in the first place. From there she could construct an escape plan.

She closed her eyes on the pillow, ignoring Vidia's high-pitched nattering. She suddenly felt the covers turn up and her eyes snapped open, seeing Vidia laying in front of her face to face. She jostled back. "Aww, aren't you cute wrapped in your blankies. Shame your daddy don't think much of you anymore." Adara's eyes blinked. Vidia began stroking the tips of her hair, "gosh, wish I had gorgeous hair like yours." Adara's insides recoiled from Vidia's fingers going through her hair. Without warning, Vidia's hand was over her face, pushing her down into the pillow, "spoilt brats don't deserve it!" Adara aimed a kick at Vidia's stomach, until she swung her other leg on the other side so that she was directly on top of Adara. The weight of Vidia was too much to push her off. With very little space, Adara tried to thump her hands into Vidia's stomach. Adara knew she would be able to if she had the strength in her. She felt her head being thrust further into the pillow, which was wet from her tears. She tried to keep her eyes open, but she was starting to lose thought and hearing.

The moment she was about to give up fighting, Adara felt the weight being lifted off of her. She tried to listen to the shouting, however, it didn't carry over the ringing in her ears as she sprung her head up from the pillow. "We don't need her anymore! She's just a liability now!"

"Get out before I throw you out!"

Adara lifted her eyelids to see Vidia narrow her eyes at Erikh, "Malum's going to know about this!"

Erikh stepped forward to match her stare, "I'll make sure to tell him first for you."

Vidia stormed out of the room, banging the door behind her. Erikh shot his eyes at Adara. He clenched his jaw and she swiped her hair back out of her face, "I never even said anything to her!" He rolled his eyes whilst turning his head side to side. "Thank you," she whispered.

Erikh's eyes snapped to Adara, who removed herself from the floor to sit on the mattress. "I wasn't going to let you die whilst Malum's not here. He would blame me otherwise."

"You're such a liar!" Erikh stared at her, moving his head back in confusion, "you're not going to let me die. You're stuck here exactly the way I am. You don't belong here and that's why I trust you."

Erikh gazed at her before shaking his head, 'I think being in the room too long has messed with your brain cells."

Adara watched him walk out, "Vidia was just trying to annoy me, right, when she spoke about my dad?"

He stopped at glanced at the clock. "I'll go and get you something to eat."

WEDNESDAY 20ᵀᴴ DECEMBER 1994

Was it possible for a person to stop thinking? Or did you have to be dead for that? Whether you're sleeping or wide awake, one thought always led to another. Would she ever stop? What was wrong with her exactly? No matter how happy she tried to be; a thought, an occurrence, something always got in the way.

When she left her mother's house. She left feeling optimistic. Hell was behind her. They couldn't hurt her any more. Even when Estella tried to get back in touch, she wasn't having any of her past back. She cut out the people that made her feel small. She left with nothing, only a small bag full of clothes. Finally, and thankfully, throughout all her hardships and because of her brilliant A Level grades she managed to get into university to do her business degree. Her results gave her hope that maybe her existence wasn't pointless. She quit her job and with her degree she got accommodation on campus.

This had to be the best part of her life. A new, perfect fresh start. New location. New people. New atmosphere. A new her. This whole new life brought her what she needed most: hope.

However, no matter how hard she had tried, her past would not leave her. Somehow, Estella continuously managed to track her down. It was non-stop phone calls.

Whilst on campus, she managed to get a sales assistant job in the university bookshop.

Bright lights and Christmas lyrics filled the air everywhere she went. Christmas was next week, so the university shop was empty. Just the random customer every hour or so. This job kept her out of the flat and helped her avoid all of Estella's phone calls. She needed to do everything in her power to keep her away from her past. She wanted to feel better and keeping her mind busy was the only way. The streets weren't leaving her memory the way she hoped.

She hated her job. It wasn't busy enough to keep her mind occupied. What was more, all her colleagues ever did was gossip. Sometimes they would look at her weirdly whilst they gossiped, and it drove her a little mad. She wanted to find a dark corner to crawl into whenever they looked at her.

London was lit with bright, sparkly red and gold Christmas decorations. Most trees were covered with tinsel and there were lights hanging from lamppost to lamppost. People were running all over the place on weekends, trying to get their family members the right gifts. The thickness of the snow meant cars were driving slower than usual, even though Londoners tried to reach home before it hit dark. Shops were now filled with chestnuts to roast and left-over Christmas baubles that no-one wanted.

There were only four days till Christmas now, so the university campus rush had died down completely. People had gone back to their families for the holidays, so the shop was decorated with bright colours specifically to trigger Robyn's annoyance. She wanted to tear down the brightness of it all. It reminded her of her Christmases from hell. Two or three times, she had experienced Christmas alone. She never minded being alone, because it meant the mean girls in the form of her mother and sister weren't around to put her down. On the other hand, loneliness came with a nasty price; thinking. She hated thinking.

Robyn brought herself back from her thoughts when she heard her name being called. The annoying, long nosed, tall colleague that existed only to gossip about her fellow lecture students was looking at her sceptically. "It's just that you're just standing behind the till..." Robyn glimpsed Helena's till that she'd been standing behind since the shop opened three hours ago. "We have customers," Helena waved her hand the way an old lady would shoo away a small puppy, "ask them if they need help." Robyn purposefully analysed the small, empty store but for the sake of getting away from Helena she walked off. Just then, a tall customer wandered in. His neat, jet-black hair wasn't gelled in place, it was naturally tidy, and it emphasised his chocolate-brown eyes. His thick black hooded coat contrasted with his obvious hereditary refinement. Helena went straight in for the attack. "Hi..." She rolled her thin blonde-haired ponytail around her fingers.

The guy placed his hands in his pockets and chewed the inside of his mouth, "I'm just here to look around."

"Well, is there anything in particular you're after?" Helena swung her leg around her other leg, appearing like she was dancing on the spot strangely.

The guy eyed her up and down before shaking his head. *Talk about driving away customers,* Robyn thought whilst making her way back to the till.

"I could swear I asked you to make yourself useful around the shop."

Robyn exhaled from the way Helena made her jump, she eyed

her straight in the face, "well Helena, I don't know if you've noticed, we've only got one customer and he's made it pretty clear he doesn't want any help."

Helena huffed, ready to respond until her eyes caught the guy approaching Robyn's till, "well, actually, can I please pay for these?"

Helena's lips perked up, "course you can darling." Her finger slithered back into her ponytail.

"Not to be rude," the temperature in the room dropped when the guy pointed at Robyn, wearing a sheepish grin. She wrapped her arms around herself even though they were already covered with her thick grey cardigan. "I was asking this lady." Helena rolled her eyes and marched away, remembering to toss her blonde ponytail in the air. Robyn picked up the books he'd placed on the counter. She squinted at the covers. "It's for my mum for Christmas, trying to get her into fantasy novels." Robyn nodded. A light murmur filled the air and she tried not to roam her eyes around the store. She heard a lady whisper the word, 'smile' in her ear and immediately her lips lifted slightly. The idea of children's fantasy novels for a mother was strange, but she didn't know why she was smiling. "Aren't you in one of my business lectures?" He asked.

"Probably." Robyn opened the bag and placed it on the counter, then took his cash.

"Allan Myers?" Robyn nodded silently, concentrating on counting. "What's your name?" Robyn's head snapped up from the cash. His features were soft, almost delicate, making her wonder if he just only turned twenty.

She blinked at the cash in her hands, trying to remember how much she had counted. After a few seconds, she bagged his books, "Robyn."

"That's a lovely name, I'm Tim." A touch of warmth approached her cheeks when he retrieved the bag from her hands. "Hope to see you again soon."

The side of Robyn's hair waved gently. She smiled again and nodded before she watched him walk out. A person actually noticed that she existed.

Sunday 24th December 1994

Christmas Eve brought snow, making the atmosphere as wintry as possible; Robyn didn't like it. The only good thing was that she didn't have any work until January. However, that meant complete loneliness. Though she was happy not to be around the gossiping girls, still it meant constant thinking. More thoughts on top of extra thoughts.

She couldn't help brooding whilst families were out enjoying the snow and handing presents to their little ones. She was on her own in her empty flat.

A breeze filtered into her small flat and she checked the window. It was closed, obviously. She would never open her window in this freezing weather. She placed her head in her hands and took deep breaths. Her thoughts on top of more thoughts were wandering around in her mind like wildfire.

BANG

Her head bolted up in the direction of the door that was swinging back and forth, wide open. She gazed at it, trying to hold off from screaming. The door was locked. A cold breeze filtered through her hair, making her heart gallop.

What was she supposed to do? She launched herself off her small single bed and placed her boots on. She grabbed her flat keys, not knowing her direction. She was just determined to not stay in her flat.

The snow was thick, and she had to lift her feet up high to keep going.

Ever since she could remember, she'd always tried to gain a peace of mind. She had become tired of trying. Yes, life was meant to have obstacles. They're there to make us stronger and to remind us of how much we can overcome. They remind us of what life is about. Why was it though, that she has had so many obstacles and no break? Was the journey meant to be this difficult?

Finding a bench, Robyn sat down and took in the view. The colourful blocks of different apartments. University, her road to happiness.

"Mind if I join you?" Robyn's eyes lifted to see the same twenty-year-old looking man from the bookshop. She shuffled to the end of the bench, not being able to find any words to leave her mouth. She felt it rude to say no, even though, truthfully, she wanted to be left alone.

"Do you remember me? I'm the one that bought those books for my mum."

Robyn nodded, "Tim." She shivered inside her big fluffy white coat.

Robyn admired the bright snow ahead of her. "Campus is strangely quiet." Robyn nodded, hoping that it stayed that way. "Got anything nice planned for tomorrow?" Robyn shook her head. "Oh." She suddenly realised that this wasn't the answer that people normally gave during Christmas. She shifted her head, noticing that he had had his eyes on her for quite a while. They were baring into her so deeply that she had to redirect her eyes back to the view, with her cheeks heated against the crispy air.

"I'm going to go and see my parents early tomorrow morning. Mum wants me home for Christmas." She didn't want to hear this. She didn't want to hear about overly doting mothers and caring fathers. Her body instantly hurled itself off the bench. She suddenly realised Tim was beside her. "Did I say something wrong?" Robyn's eyes widened in response. "So, why walk off?"

The rush of the wind flew through her hair. She squinted, noticing a different sensation of chilly air brush past her cheek. Something was in front of her, she could feel it. It felt like she was standing next to a massive block of ice. She suddenly caught a light echo, "don't walk away." Her brown pupils expanded upon hearing that familiar voice overtake her ears. She concentrated on her hands so that Tim couldn't see her bottom lip quivering.

"It's cold." Robyn saw Tim's eyebrows crease in thinking of a response. "Merry Christmas, Tim."

She plunged her small feet in and out of the thick snow quickly without looking back.

TUESDAY 17TH JANUARY 1995

The new year began. The snow still gave chilly, short days with long evenings. The dread of work didn't outweigh her excitement for her new lectures. She loved her lectures. It was important for her to focus on the subject at hand. She was determined to gain a first: she wanted to prove to herself her own worth. To know she was good at something. It was Tuesday morning, her first lecture of the week. She was five minutes early and the first one to arrive. Robyn heard the door swing open. She was too lost in her doodling on the corner of her lined paper to see who it was.

"Nice," Robyn jumped a tad in her chair. Was he stalking her or something? "I'm beginning to find it strange that we keep meeting." He placed himself in the seat next to her. She contained the urge to get up and walk away. "Am I that ugly?" He asked, curiously with a slight grin.

"Sorry?" Robyn's eyes broadened. "You seem to find it hard to look at me." Her head tilted; if anything, she found him the complete opposite. The lines in his face were soft and his brown eyes were completely tranquil, showing her he was never in a rush to go anywhere. "You don't like talking much, do you?" Robyn bit the inside of her mouth; she agreed, the sudden encounters were weird.

People eventually started piling in. The lecture began, and Robyn was grateful to find an excuse to not talk to Tim. He wasn't a bad guy. She just found talking to him odd. What was she supposed to say to him? That she had no father? Her mother for some reason hated her and decided to throw her out and make her homeless? She thought her only sibling was the devil in human form and that she has no friends? That could trigger an interesting reaction. Robyn caught all of the lecturer's notes, knowing Tim's eyes were boring into her from the side.

As she tried to understand what the lecturer was saying, Robyn saw a note slide in front of her. She stared at it, unable to register the moment taking place. Her heartbeat picked up slightly whilst she swallowed. A whisper hung in the air around her, telling her to answer. She reluctantly brought the note in front of her with her lips pressed together.

Where abouts in London are you from?

That seemed like a perfectly simple question to Robyn. She answered 'Brentford' and within seconds he slid the note back.

I'm from Kensington. How you finding uni so far?

Robyn's large eyes blinked at the note like she'd been asked the exact number of the planet's population. She stared at the note for a while before a cold voice nipped at her ears. She blinked again before scanning the lecture room. The lecturer was still talking loudly, she breathed deeply, staring at him. She read the note again and felt Tim's eyes on her before she heard the airy voice telling her to be honest. She picked up the pen.

Kensington is a nice area. It's okay.

Tim giggled quietly at the reply and eventually wrote back saying:

It's alright I guess. It's popular. Did you enjoy Christmas?

Robyn read the note, thinking that Christmas was lonely, freezing and boring. *Be honest,* the voice chiming in her ears reminded her again.

It was a typical Christmas.

Within seconds, Robyn received his reply:

Let's aim to make your Christmas better next year then.

Robyn knew something was glowing around her. She beamed at the note.

Wednesday 22ⁿᵈ February 1995

Her eyes scanned the international business book in front of her. She highlighted some of the definitions in yellow that she knew she had to take note of at some point before she forgot them. Keeping her large, brown eyes on her book she drifted her right arm over the table. The clink of heavy dishes from the kitchen resonated throughout the bright red canteen reminding her of where she was. The scent of lunch took over the canteen during the bitter February day. Robyn was content with her warm coffee whilst rain pounded at the windows of the empty space. She, for some reason, had never felt so comfortable. This was her home now. She felt safe.

She was about to raise her hand to reach her cup, but instead the white paper cup was placed in front of her. Her eyes flickered up and she gulped.

"Sorry, thought I'd help you out."

She took a deep breath, "thanks." He pointed at the seat beside her and she closed her book with a nod. She wrapped her hands around her warm coffee cup, knowing that they were going to get into conversation. The past month, Tim had made the effort of sitting next to her in their lectures. He always left a sparkle in her eyes, making her days seem brighter for the past few dull weeks. One hand ruffled his neat hair whilst the other dropped his bag down with a light thud.

"Just came back from seeing my family," he said. She dropped her head and took a deep breath. "My mum goes all nutty when she sees me."

She didn't want to hear this, so she took a deep breath and opened her book. "You're always on campus studying or working," Tim teased.

She lifted her head up to him. She swiped her glowing blonde hair behind her shoulders so that it was out the way, "I keep to myself."

"No family?" He leaned into the table, searing his eyes into her.

She bit her lip, blinking at her book. "Dad died."

He nodded, "mother?" She glanced at her book again. A sudden chill that she had become used to overtook her surroundings. "Brothers or sisters?" She took a deep breath, thinking of Estella and a fire entered her chest. She bit her tongue, whilst her eyes flickered, trying to ignore all the memories that seeped into the front of her mind. Tim cleared his throat, bringing her back to the present, "would you like help studying?"

That familiar, soft nippy voice, which had been guiding her for the past few months whispered in her ear. She passed her book over to him and he grinned before retrieving some books from his bag, "do you want a warmer coffee first?"

Her eyes grew wide at the sound of a giggle leaving her smiling mouth.

Friday 1st December 1995

Robyn was in complete, colourful heaven. She passed her first year with flying colours and Tim had annoyed the hell out of her before she finally gave in. He took her to watch a movie and then dinner after. The movie was as horrendous as the dinner was lovely, the whole day made her feel young. It made her feel her age. She was doing something other people do. She was talking to someone and that person was responding to her answers and to her actions. She felt like she was actually here to be happy. She had never genuinely smiled and laughed in all her years until she was with him. After a while, they relocated to a small flat together near the campus.

Robyn sat on their old grey sofa, watching Tim decorate their small, green Christmas tree. She had lied to him and told him that her family never celebrated Christmas. The truth was, Estella and their mother always went abroad every time Christmas came, leaving Robyn alone in the house for two weeks. She had never had a real Christmas. It was the first time she had anticipated its arrival, because she wasn't alone this year. Tim was on a mission to make it a memorable Christmas.

Robyn had only told Tim bits of her history with the truth of her father. She didn't mention her sister and mother. She always used the wholesome word, 'family' when referring to the both of them rather than individually. Keeping her past at bay was hard, however, she managed it. Tim happened to be more of an 'in the moment' person rather than latching on to someone's history, which could quite possibly never affect their present. She just hoped it stayed this way.

He hung the last green bauble on the tree, then looked to her with his chocolate-coloured button eyes, "what do you think?"

She tilted her head, examining the small, multicoloured tree that sat on the side coffee table. "It's bright." He squinted his eyes, making her giggle, "it's perfect."

His lips lifted with his legs ready to run at her, until the sound of the phone stopped him. She heard the word 'mum' and she bolted from the sofa to make her way to the bathroom. She sat down on the white marble floor, waiting for the conversation to end. She wanted to shout at herself for moments like this. Every instinct pulled her away whenever he wanted to give her the phone, making her feel childish. The light knocks on the door came and she knew she had to stop behaving like a child and leave the bathroom.

There was something soft at the back of her head that startled her when she dipped her head down, ready to swing it back into the wall. She stared at the place she had been sitting. Her breathing picked up slightly. Her lips quivered and she squeaked with the intention of screaming. She felt a heavy shift around her. A tingle brushed against her hand and her breathing halted. She recognised the chill and she shivered, causing her to wrap her arms around herself. The light breeze hovered at her ear. "It's okay." The door swung open in front of her and she stood staring at the living room before cautiously moving her feet ahead.

Their rented flat kitchen contained cupboards that needed fixing and a chipped work surface that needed replacing. The whole flat was outdated and dull; still, she liked it. The flat called her, and she enjoyed inhabiting it. This was where Tim and she belonged. It was their home.

Tim stood still in the kitchen corner, pouring himself a tea, "Mum wanted to speak to you?" She pointed at the bathroom, wanting to say something. He just nodded before he placed her cup on the other end of the counter. She took slow steps, approaching the kitchen knowing he was watching her. She reached the counter and wrapped her fingers around the mug like it was her shield. "Robyn," her eyes raised up from her mug. His acorn eyes bore into her before removing his hands from his mug and enveloping hers, which were still holding her mug. She felt the heat against her palm from both the mug and his hands. The gesture made a rush of air slowly sweep through her lungs in an unexpected sense of relief. Tim bit his lip and stared at her, "would you be okay with meeting my parents next year?"

Robyn's eyes bulged open upon hearing his words. She wanted to clutch onto her chest. He wasn't forcing her; she knew though, that he wanted her to say that she was okay with the idea. What he didn't know was that these people wouldn't care about her. Only Tim did, and that was all she wanted.

FRIDAY 17TH FEBRUARY 2012

It had been a few days since Robyn had seen Estella. She hadn't gone into work for a while and knew for sure she was eventually going to be fired. The truth was though, she didn't care. She hated her job and she hated the people. People that were always trying to be nice and perfect. She knew very well that there was always an ulterior motive to their niceness. They always wanted something; she just could never understand what. She was surrounded by these types of people all the time.

She hadn't left her bed in two days. Her mind felt separate from her body and her body felt separate from her emotions. She was trying to hold the three together, when all she wanted was a real night's worth of sleep and for everything to just stop for at least just a little while.

A tapping noise resonated from the living room that made her wet eyes spring open. She was about to close them again, until the tapping grew louder. Her insides trembled and her breathing halted. She dragged her heavy legs off the bed after her two long days of digging further and further into her blankets. Though she noticed how cold she'd been, it suddenly occurred to her that flat felt like a freezer. She swept her muggy blonde hair out of her face before she took a few steps out of her bedroom and into the living room.

She walked in a few further steps, noticing something different on her wall. A picture that wasn't there before. She stepped in front of the picture and her eyes sprang open. Her legs wobbled, seeing the picture of Estella and her. Estella was just a baby lying in her small arms.

"You're both so beautiful." Robyn froze on the spot, recognising that voice; that same voice that had been ringing in her ears for the past few years. Her thoughts scrambled and her hands flew to her head. She felt like bricks were going to crumble above her. She slowly rotated her body around, ignoring the sparring thoughts in her mind.

The brilliant, light-filled vision in front of her knocked her breath away before her legs thudded to the floor. Nayla was hanging above her with her blonde hair strapped back in a wavy ponytail.

Her dark blue, flowery top unleashed a whizz of memories that trailed through her mind. Robyn's eyes fixated on her mother, refusing to register her presence. Her lips quivered, while her hands pulled at her unwashed hair, trying to comprehend her mother's unusual, thin-lipped smile. Nayla wasn't radiating her common aura of anger and frustration; in fact, she was completely serene. The atmosphere felt like glittering fairies were flying around everywhere. Nayla gleamed her red, smiling lips before she faded from sight.

Monday 20th February 2012

Robyn heard her flat door open and heard her name being called. She recognised the voice, wondering if it was ever going to leave her alone. She heard the room door open a few seconds later. Robyn saw a bag of chips and a glass of vodka being placed in front of her. "I nicked Tim's keys. He'll get annoyed, but I don't care." The smell of the salty, greasy chips took over her senses and without thinking she picked up a chip. The heat suddenly filled her insides with complete warmth.
"Robyn." Clare said lightly. She kept her eyes on the bag of chips while chewing, "you know why I decided to go into social work?" Robyn blinked at her drink, knowing Clare was waiting for her to say something. "My sister." Robyn glimpsed up at Clare, whose green eyes rested on her; she had to turn away from her stare. "The last time I spoke to Kelci, she was so upset. She wouldn't tell me why and I thought if she wanted to tell me she would, but then the next thing I knew, she was gone. So, I promised myself that I'd do everything in my power to help others the way that my sister had always helped me. Even if it means sitting there silently waiting for a response from them, because I don't want someone's else's life being snatched the way my sister's was." Robyn sipped her vodka, she felt the polished taste swim down her and ignite a small spark. "What I think people like Kris, Tim and so many others forget is that every person deals with things differently. Whether it is talking too much, or completely shutting down. People that don't understand aren't bad though Robyn, it's just the way they are; but, we can only help them to understand. Babies aren't born with the emotions that we have Robyn, emotions are always created and stem from somewhere. But…"
"What did you do when your sister died?" Clare's electric eyes fluttered at Robyn, trying not to appear surprised that she'd

spoken. Robyn went back to facing the bag of chips, whilst picking up the bottle of vodka and pouring some in for herself.

"I blamed Kris for everything." Robyn inhaled, not knowing what to say, "I wanted to go to his house and hurt him. I remember I was so angry, and that was all I felt for so many years after she died. I came up with so many different scenarios in my head that made him appear villainous. He came around one day, and I couldn't even face looking at him. I started off angry, but when he tried to talk me, I realised I wasn't angry at him, he was just the object I was taking my anger out on. I was angry with myself, because I felt like I'd failed Kelci in some way."

"How did you accept it?" Robyn asked quietly.

Robyn stared at Clare's watering green eyes. "I don't really know, to be honest. I think acceptance comes slowly when you allow people to come through the walls that you've built around you. Because if you don't, those walls are going to be there forever, and loneliness will overtake you. And that's the worst. Loneliness is the worst. Because you think things to yourself that you don't want to be thinking. By talking to others, you can think out loud, and the words of others are there to challenge the thoughts you shouldn't be thinking."

Robyn raised the bottle to Clare, and she nodded. She poured some in her glass and pushed the chips near her. Clare sipped and then coughed, "oh gosh, I'll stick to wine," she picked up a chip and quickly chewed. Robyn focused her bambi like eyes at Clare. Was the alcohol influencing her to suddenly want to talk, or was it that Clare was describing everything she was suffering?

"Does Tim know you're here?" Clare swung her head side to side, the chip visibly sliding down her throat. "How did Estella find out where I was?"

"Kris went to a restaurant a while ago and the waitress said what her name was. You mentioned your name in front of Tim, and they put two and two together. Kris went back and spoke to her and gave her your address." Robyn ground her teeth. "He didn't do this to hurt you, Robyn. Just like him, we know when you need support around you."

Robyn rolled her eyes, "I don't need her. My half-sister is a two-faced, cunning bitch."

"You do need her. I don't know what happened between the two of you, but there's no time like the present to try and make things work. And if she's still a two-faced bitch, well, you have me." Robyn felt a wave float through her. Tears spilled down her face. Her hand rested on her chest, trying to catch up with her breathing. She saw the chips move back and Clare sat in front of her, taking Robyn's hands in hers. "I know it's none of my business, but if you want to talk to me, you can and if you don't, that's absolutely fine. But if Estella came knocking on your door, that means she cares. Now is the time to change things, Robyn. You don't have to feel the way you do. No one does. I'm your friend. Let me help you. I promise you Robyn, you can trust me."

After a few minutes passed, Clare got up and opened the curtains. The rush of the blaring sunlight hit all corners of the room. Robyn covered her eyes from the bright glare.

~

Robyn sat in her bath. The piping hot water hit at all parts of her skin, chipping away at her aches and pains. She just hoped they didn't reform when she left the bath. She dipped her head into the water and allowed the heat to reach the tip of her hairline. After a few seconds, she swung her head back up to the edge of the bath. She could feel the tears leaving her eyes.

She didn't understand what had happened. She could hear Clare pottering around in her apartment. Should she trust her? She had already lost so much though, so, what was she risking in trying to trust her? She hadn't spoken to someone so openly in such a long time. How did Clare do that? How did Clare make her talk? Was she manipulating her? She had made promises though. She was going to break them, they all did. Without thinking, Robyn jumped out of her bath.

She got dressed and walked into her room. She blinked. Everything was tidied. Her bed was made. She could see her carpet. There were no glasses on her bedside table. Robyn made her way into the living room. There were no dishes visible on the kitchen counter. Clare had covered her ripped sofa with a blanket. All signs of her mental state were removed from her flat.

Clare approached her and took her hand slowly to seat her at the table, where there was a notebook and pencil. Clare sat down next to her and Robyn glanced at Clare, then back at the notepad. "This isn't going to be an overnight thing, Robyn. It's going to take time."

THURSDAY 23RD FEBRUARY 2012

Robyn sat on her living room floor with the picture of herself and her sister in front of her. The room was filled with only the sound of her thoughts. Her time with Clare had surprised her. She was now starting to become accepting of Clare's company. Clare had been visiting her more and more over the past few weeks, and Robyn was beginning to open up to her. It seemed Clare wanted to be her friend; an actual friend, who cared for her. Sometimes it did plague her though; was this some massive joke to make fun of her? Was Estella in on it?

She rested her head back on the sofa seat and crossed her legs on the floor. She closed her eyes and the vision of her mother entered her mind. Her eyes sprang open remembering that chilliness and her strange smile. A smile that her mother had never given her; something she'd been deprived of all her life. It wasn't real. It can't have been, because she was dead. Estella had made that clear. Her mother was dead. How could she randomly appear before her anyway? It didn't make any sense.

She decided to listen to Clare. She pushed her shoulders back and closed her eyes. She slowed her breathing down and inhaled through her nose. She focused her thoughts on her senses; things she could hear, feel, smell and taste. There were no sounds; just complete, still, silence. It was just the echoes of people nattering outside her flat that she shut out. She traced her skin with her hands and it felt soft. Her head felt overloaded, as though she was holding heavy irons rods. She knew the rods were her continuously circling thoughts. No matter how much she wanted to drop the weight, she kept holding them up. Her upper back ached from her slumped down shoulders. She attempted to remain focused on her senses, even though her right shoulder called to be clicked for the millionth time. She could smell lavender air freshener. The spray ones that you could plug in; they kept making a puffing sound every hour or so. She hadn't eaten much today, so her mouth felt dry.

The air ran through her nostrils and she held it for a few seconds before exhaling it slowly out through her mouth. She felt a few strands of her blonde hair wave and her eyes popped open. A chill tingled against her bare arms and she realised she was experiencing that same chilly sensation again. She scanned the room eagerly for an answer. Her eyes then moved behind her to hover over the kitchen and then back to the television again. She breathed in, sensing that she wasn't alone.

She took in another breath, brushing back her freshly washed hair out of her face.

"Robyn." Her eyes sprang open. Her mother was hovering next to her, with crossed legs, bathed in a glowing light. The air was knocked out of her system, making her cough. She pulled herself back, dragging her legs without letting her eyes leave the sight of her beaming mother.

"It's okay." Robyn jumped up on her feet, draping her arms around herself. "You've grown up so much," her mother said.

Robyn blinked at her before she began shaking her head, "no, no! You're dead!" She bolted to her bedroom and slammed the door behind her. She spun around, aiming to get back into her covers, but instead there was Nayla hovering beside her bed, with her beaming eyes and sharp jawline. Tears dripped down Robyn's cheeks and she heard her own heartbeat galloping. She wondered whether to run out of the flat. Her feet halted, and she turned to see her mother a few feet behind her.

"Robyn, it's okay. I'm dead, darling." Robyn's hands began shaking. Nayla pointed at the sofa, "I know you're scared. Sit down." Robyn's feet remained fixed in position, remembering the cycle of breathing Clare advised. "You're confused, sweetie. I understand that. Let me explain."

"Why are you talking to me like that?" Nayla dropped her head whilst hovering up and down on the spot. Robyn made a cautious step towards her mother. "You're dead, but if you're here that would make you a ghost."

Nayla lifted her head and nodded, "I've been around for years. I just didn't know when the best time would be to show myself."

"And why is the best time now?"

"Because life has brought you some amazing opportunities and I don't want to you to ignore them."

Robyn massaged her thumping head, "why do you care?" Nayla hovered closer to Robyn, who didn't move. Robyn rubbed her fingers at the sides of her temple, "I've just found out you're not even my mother. That's why you treated me so horribly. Why didn't you just give me away?" Nayla's lips stammered, seeing Robyn drop her head in hands.

"Oh my."

Robyn whirled around for the front door, and Nayla cried out, "no wait! Please!"

Robyn halted, directing her large, piercing eyes at her mother.

"I know that of all the ghosts that exist on this planet I'm the last you would want to be seeing, but I can't leave unless we've spoken."

"Well, we've spoken, and I think that's already more than what my brain can process."

"Robyn, I treated you so badly! I took out all my anger towards your father on you." Robyn's eyes widened and her hands were balled into fists. She felt her chest close and her breathing stagger. Nayla bit her lips before she continued, "I didn't want to put you into care or something, because I thought that I could raise you like my own, but seeing the way you grew up, you reminded me more and more of your father. I didn't realise how bitter I was. And I was embarrassed. Embarrassed about what your father did to me. So, giving you away in front of others would only show my embarrassment. I'm so sorry."

"You're sorry." Robyn's bottom lips quivered. Tears sprang from her eyes and down her red cheeks. She took in a deep breath, "sorry." Robyn repeated the word, grasping the meaning behind it.

"Robyn, I had bottled up so much anger." Nayla moved her hands in and out of each other, "so much anger. And it came out at you. I've never been able to forgive myself for that. So, when I realised that I couldn't move on, I stayed with you." Robyn slowly lifted her large, wet eyes at her mother, "I've been with you the whole-time sweetie. When you were in uni, I was there. Guiding you."

Robyn placed her hands over her ears in an attempt to drown out her mother's unrecognisably kind voice. A gentle voice that was once filled with vicious threats that took over the thoughts of her fear-riddled mind for years. She couldn't handle that distortion any longer. More tears trailed down her heated cheeks like rivers. Nayla hovered closer and her face immediately shook. Robyn dropped her hands from her ears to wave them defensively.

"Please, Robyn. I just want to help you. That's what I've been trying to do for the past few years. I want to help you."

Robyn pursed her lips, "guilt."

Nayla nodded, "and shame." Robyn dropped her head, seeing Nayla hover closer from the corner of her eyes, "ashamed of the way I treated you. I punished you for what your father did to me. That was wrong. You were just an innocent child."

Robyn swiped her hair away from her face, taking in the breeze around her and Nayla continued whispering, "I am so sorry."

Robyn felt the air swimming in and out of her so fast that she made her way to the sofa with her hands quaking. Her weight dipped into the cushion and she dropped her head back. She blinked, seeing her past flash through her mind, reliving all her memories. "Tim has been good for you." Her eyes whizzed to her mother, "I'm so glad you found him." Robyn crossed her legs and placed her head in her hands, "and I'm glad you found Clare, too." She felt a chilly rush of air sweep across her and then her mother was kneeling in front of her. Nayla's caring demeanour took her breath away and she leaned back slightly, away from her icy-cool aura, "Robyn, life is handing you doors to open. Please don't keep them shut. I'm culpable for the heavy and painful heart you have now, so, please take my advice to heal it. Let Clare help you."

Robyn couldn't stop herself from sobbing out loud. She couldn't comprehend if the chilly figure in front of her was truly her mother. Was she dreaming this? She closed her eyes and let the heavy thoughts drop her head back onto the sofa, "my real mother didn't want me."

"She had met someone else. She just upped and left because she had met someone else. But she died a year or so after. She had committed suicide." Robyn picked her head up, creasing her eyebrows at Nayla. "I guess guilt can overtake a person."

Robyn bit her bottom lip, with tears filtering down her face. The chill from the figure in front of her contrasted with her burning cheeks. The arms of the mother she had craved so long; the kind, comforting, loving words she longed for were now in front of her. Her body shivered and her thoughts jumped up and down in her mind. She felt a piercing rod strike right through her head. Her eyes swivelled around the room.

"Robyn." She then felt the nippy touch against her burning red cheek. Robyn flinched, before her body rested deeper into the cushion. Her mind slowed, registering the first act of love from the mother that took her in. "I created such hardship in your life, Robyn, but you can change that. You're strong. You're capable of anything. You're so bright and clever. You're not alone. Trust Clare. Her intentions are good and honest." Robyn inhaled the coldness around her, "and please give Estella a chance." Robyn's eyes shot towards her mother, unable to stop her teeth from grinding. "Please. Don't push her away because of me. She cares for you so deeply."

She dipped further into the sofa with tears streaming down her face. The icy, although caressing touch on her forehead forced her eyelids to drop into a deep sleep.

Part Three

Tuesday 10th April 2012

Kris had invited everyone around for the evening. Even Clare. On the occasions he had tried to go and see her, she hadn't been home. He'd tried texting and ringing her, only to be ignored countless times. He dropped her a message that morning for the last time, hoping she wouldn't ignore it.

Reva was on her holidays again and he had had her in the office a couple of times. Adara couldn't ignore it when her daughter would run off from her friend's house. The thought of Reva lost on the street caused fear deeper than her current anger against him. So, Adara would sometimes drop Reva at Kris's workplace in the morning and she would spend the day with Lauren. Kris had attempted messaging Adara twice, he wasn't going to try anymore. She had to come around in her own time. Kris just wished she would hurry up and drop her stubbornness, because her stubborn-natured morning visits were beginning to irritate him. Today, having left work early, Kris bought Reva home.

Kris wasn't the best cook, but neither was he a bad cook. That's what he hoped anyway. He stuck to the simple things today, hoping that nothing would go wrong. He ripped open the packet of couscous. "You haven't got any movies." Kris paused, seeing Reva standing with her arms crossed, "what are you going to do tonight if you don't have any movies?"

Kris smiled, "we talk, Reva. Like people did when there was no technology."

"You sound like an old person." Kris gaped at her, watching her walk back out of the kitchen.

After pouring hot water onto the couscous, he made himself a coffee and Reva a hot chocolate, before making his way into the living room. She wasn't there. Kris placed the two mugs down on the table and went into the dining room. He shouted for her, but only the clicking clocks in the house could be heard. He went into the garden and searched the back. He rubbed the back of his neck and then made his way up the stairs whilst he shouted for her again.

"In here, Kris!" Kris blinked at his bedroom door and opened it.

He swallowed upon seeing what she was looking through. "This is lovely." He glimpsed at his cupboard, seeing the doors were shut. He had placed that box high up; she surely couldn't have reached it. He rubbed his hand through his hair and took a deep breath before placing himself down on the floor next to Reva.

"Your wife was really beautiful."

Kris nodded. He interlocked his fingers, worried he might snatch the book from her like a nursery child. She flipped the page over to show a picture of Kris at a school where Kelci had made him give a talk. He dropped his eyes from the album whilst Reva concentrated on the pictures in the book, "Reva, where did you find this?"

"It was on your bed." Kris rubbed the base of his neck, knowing he didn't leave this laying on his bed. He hadn't removed this book from his cupboard in years.

Something stopped him from telling Reva to leave the book and go downstairs. He listened to the silence. The clocks. Reva's steady breathing. The pages turning. The subtle beeping from one of the house alarms. His wife's ringing giggle. He squeezed his eyes shut, seeing Kelci appear in the forefront of his mind. She was wearing her cream top, sitting on the bed and rubbing her arm. Her lashes fluttered back and forth from him to the book. *She was worried I wouldn't like the book,* Kris thought.

He opened his eyes, "do you mind if I see something?" He asked. Reva shifted the book over with her small hand.

He flipped to the back of the book to the note Kelci had written for him. The words had changed though:

Don't look back Kris. Stay present to move forward. I am always here for you. Never forget that. I will be with you everywhere you go.

Kelci's silky voice was back in his ears again. "Look forward, Kris." He placed his finger over her curly handwriting and bit the inside of his mouth.

Kris exhaled and flipped back to the beginning before sliding it back to Reva, "I'm going to go check the chicken before I set the house on fire." He ran downstairs with the intention of opening the door to the grill, instead he rested his hands on the counter and bent his head down, pacing his breaths. He heard his phone beep, knowing who the message was from: Adara, telling him she'd be there after six. He resisted the urge to throw his phone on the kitchen counter before making his way into the family room for his coffee.

After a few minutes, Reva came and sat opposite him on the sofa. Kris glanced at her tucking short strands of her bob behind her small ears. He could feel her brown eyes analysing him and debating, before she asked suddenly, "how come you have no children?"

Kris choked on his sip of coffee. He hastily placed his mug down, "you ask the most random questions for a child." Reva stared at him. He blinked at his mug before rubbing the base of his neck. "We were really young, Reva."

"My mum and dad were young when they had me." Kris looked at her, "my Dad was great. He used to play with me a lot whilst the other kids went to school." Kris placed his mug on the table in order to pay full attention to the way her words were forming. "I don't know how he died. But when we came here, we moved around a lot until mum got the house. Then she started sending me to school." Reva stared down at her hot chocolate and tucked her hands underneath her thighs, "I don't like school much." Reva gazed around the house before her eyes stopped at some of the pictures on top of the bar.

"I didn't like school much either." Her eyes blinked back to him. "I couldn't find a group of friends that I really liked, and I found most of the subjects boring."

"I only have one friend in school." Kris nodded, waiting for her to continue, "she's the only one that doesn't say anything to me for not understanding things when the teacher tells us stuff."

Kris chewed the inside of his mouth trying to not grind his teeth, "and what stuff doesn't she say that the others do?" Reva stared at her hot chocolate. "Do you speak to your teacher when someone says something to you?" Reva's eyes dropped down to her knees. "What about your mum?" Reva's hair swung side to side, "why haven't you told your mum?" She shrugged her shoulders. "Don't you think your mum would want to know if you're not happy at school?" Reva picked up her hot chocolate and began sipping it.

Kris stared at her, not knowing what to say. He had told her the truth. He never liked school. Though he never felt like he fit in anywhere, no one ever said anything to him. Other kids enjoyed playing on the grounds, kicking the ball around or sitting in groups, laughing about things that he had very little interest in: games, television, films and sports. School was like a chore for him that he managed to get through, however, for Reva it was a complete struggle because others were making it clear she didn't fit in. He took a deep breath and rubbed his hands over his face, recognising a thread circling his chest and bricks falling on his shoulders. Reva glanced at him and he returned her a strained smile, "drink your hot chocolate." She nodded when he heard the doorbell rang. He wanted to tell her to stand up for herself and not let people put her down. He was unsure of how to use his words though, just in case she ended up in trouble on the playground.

Aunt Louise stood at the door when he opened it, wearing her bright red smile and long red coat over a pink dress. He peered at her hands and pursed his lips. "no harm in me helping," she said, raising the dish.

"No, just offending my hospitality." Kris rolled his eyes, watching his aunt march straight into his kitchen.

Reva was still sitting on the sofa when Aunt Louise walked through. Aunt Louise's face beamed whilst she tilted her head. Reva jumped from the sofa and faced her with a toothy smile. Kris grinned, wondering what was going through Aunt Louise's brain. She bent down slightly, analysing Reva's demeanour before Reva put her hand out, introducing herself. Aunt Louise took her hand and beamed at her, "oh aren't you just a gem!" When she sat down to talk, Kris took the opportunity to grab Aunt Louise a glass of wine and place it on the table in front of her. The moment Reva ran into the kitchen to put her mug away, Aunt Louise gazed at him. Kris explained how he met Reva and Adara and she wrinkled her long thin eyebrows, "and after meeting you in a park she just happens to trust you with her child?"

Kris moved his head back, "do I look like I'm not trustworthy?" Aunt Louise hit the side of his leg and tutted. Reva appeared in front of them on the sofa and began talking to Aunt Louise again. A thought popped into his head about whether to tell Aunt Louise about Tim and Clare. He knew this would infuriate Tim, it was for Clare's sake he felt burdened. Kris sighed, thinking Aunt Louise didn't even know Tim and Robyn had broken up. He rubbed his head at the high school drama forming around him. He heard the front door click open and then shut.

Tim walked into the living room and greeted his mother. Reva stared at him, "I haven't seen you in any of the pictures." Tim eyed Kris questioningly before clearing his throat.

Kris chuckled, seeing Aunt Louise introduce Tim to Reva. "Oh, you're the little girl Lauren won't stop going on about."

Reva placed her hands underneath her chin and tilted her head slightly with a grin, "office helper, Lauren calls me."

Tim and Aunt Louise burst out laughing, making Kris shake his head, "please don't say that to anyone else Reva." He thought of all the paperwork he would have to deal with if he ever had a lawsuit filed against him for child labour. Kris's phone beeped and he read the message from Adara telling him she would be here soon. This meant she wanted Reva ready to jump out of the house so that she didn't have to come to the door. Adara was beginning to treat him like a babysitter; he didn't appreciate it. Kris rolled his eyes. He rushed into the kitchen and threw his blackberry on the counter, hoping in the back of his mind that he hadn't broken any part of it.

"You seem stressed," Tim said, from where he was standing on the other side of the kitchen. "is it the girl's mother?" Tim scratched his head, "Lauren said you had a bit of a thing for her." Kris exhaled from the weight of more bricks being tossed on his shoulders. He was being pulled in different directions and didn't know which part of his life to deal with first. Should he bother with Adara? Was it his responsibility to help Reva? Then, every moment of the day Kris was worried Tim was introducing Clare to his father. Kris rubbed his head and exhaled again. "Kris, talk to me."

"I think Reva's being picked on in school."

Tim blinked and placed his hands in his pockets, "bullied?" Kris rubbed the back of his neck, realising that if something wasn't done about this it, it could lead to bullying. The circle of threads in him suddenly twisted into a knot. "Are you going to tell the mother?"

Kris suddenly felt like his head was on fire. "Do you know what Tim?" He grabbed his hair and pulled at it before letting it go, "Adara is flipping crazy. One minute she's telling me about her family, then the next she shuts down, then the next I feel like she's going to tear me down completely if I try to speak to her! I don't know where I'm at with her. And what's stupid is that I hardly know her and yet she drops Reva off all the time like I'm her bloody babysitter…" Kris bit his tongue, "…not that I mind, but I feel like I know the child better than the mother. I don't know what she wants. What's more pathetic is that I've only known her for a few months, and she makes me mad like I've been in a relationship with her for like a year! How the hell does that make sense?!"

Tim leaned against the counter, biting his bottom lip, "I feel like you've had that bottled up inside you for quite a while." Kris took a deep breath, placing his fingers against his temple. "Kris, I'm not going to give you advice about Reva confiding in you, because you already know what you need to do. In terms of Adara, it's simple, first deal with Reva's issue then figure out later if you feel it's worth you sticking around for all the aggravation." Kris watched Tim walk out in a daze. The problem was he didn't know how to walk away even if he wanted to.

Kris began sorting the snacks into different bowls. A few seconds later, he heard nattering. His eyes widened when he saw Tim drag Clare into the kitchen by her arm. "You wouldn't believe who the hell she's gone and brought." Tim let go of her and she stood with her arms crossed, rolling her eyes at the way Tim was pointing at her like she was a troublesome teenager. Kris stared at Clare, downplaying his surprise. "I don't have super vision Tim, you're going to have to tell me."

Clare stomped her foot, "Robyn isn't a serial killer, Tim." Kris didn't want to be a part of this conversation. He looked at the snacks on the counter, debating whether he regretted this gathering; he didn't want to bring any drama into his house.

"Tell her!" Tim said, startling Kris, "she went to the flat without asking me!"

Clare's eyes flew open, revealing every millimetre of her electric green irises. Kris placed his hand over his mouth, trying not to laugh. "Tell her!?" Clare faced Tim with her knuckles formed into fists, "I'm not a child. You don't tell me what to do! I do what I want to do!"

Tim puffed at Kris, "why the hell aren't you saying anything!?" He gestured around the kitchen, throwing his arms around, "this is your house."

Kris rubbed the back of his neck, suddenly feeling like piggy in the middle, "to be honest Tim, if Kelci were here she'd say any friend of Clare's is a friend of hers." Clare raised her head up, showing her teeth with a wide grin. Tim's shoulders dropped. "Tim, you're acting like Robyn is a psychotic killer. She's not. She's angry. And besides, wouldn't you prefer that they both got along rather than wrap wires around each other's necks?" Kris shot his eyes directly at Tim and raised his eyebrows. Tim rolled his eyes before walking out of the kitchen.

Clare stared at Kris. "Lauren came to see me this morning." Kris's eyes widened at Clare from the thought of what Lauren might have said to her. Clare crossed her arms and breathed in, "Kris I meant it when I said I'm not a child. I know a complete creep when I see one and at most of the parties you had, Kelci made it clear that she didn't like him without having to say anything to me." Kris rubbed his head, exhaling deeply, "you don't have to worry about me." He nodded, before Clare wrapped her arms around him. He hugged her back and placed a kiss on her head. "Now you can tell me who that little girl is."

THURSDAY 13TH SEPTEMBER 1994

Hope had come her way a little when Erikh came into her room with a black blindfold. Everyone had disappeared and he gave her the chance to do the same. They were sitting under a large tree; Erikh's gaze focused beyond the field.

The crisp air prickled at her dry skin and Erikh had given her his thick jacket to wrap herself in. She enjoyed the scent of freshly dried grass after a light shower of rain. The scent tingled in her nose and she smiled, feeling alive. There were trees beyond trees that sat beneath a blanket of glittering darkness. If she was still in England, she had never found the country so captivating.

Erikh cleared his throat and it pulled her out of her trance. He was staring at the trees. "What are you thinking?" She asked. He shrugged.

Adara watched him rip at the grass before brushing his curtained hair away from his eyes. She appreciated the risk he had taken to bring her out before and she still appreciated it now. His thought process was important, and she was curious. She was still eager to know the words dominating his mind. He was an intriguing person. Unlike the others, she noticed how he kept to himself and hardly ever threatened her. He was just full of warnings and advice.

Adara could feel hardships radiating from him and wanted to know what they were. She instead decided to keep the conversation light. "Imagine having a name like tree, or something." Erikh's eyebrows lifted slightly. She showed her teeth in response to his confused expression at her comment before he went back to staring at the field. "You don't think?" She asked, attempting to continue the random topic.

Erikh shook his head and blinked, keeping his attention on the field ahead of him, "I never really thought about it Adara."

She blinked, "...think about it." He took a deep breath, "Erikh Tree."

He dropped his head, rubbing his temple. Adara hoped that she had finally got through to his sense of humour, "fields."

Adara's raised her eyebrows, "what?"

"My last name is Fields." Adara's lips formed a small 'o' and she dipped her head into the musky scent of his warm jacket.

She shrugged her shoulders, "Erikh Fields... well at least it isn't tree. Imagine saying *that* to people."

Erikh's chest went up and then dropped with a heavy sigh, "is this topic going anywhere?"

Adara went silent, snuggling her head back in the jacket in defeat. Silence passed with only the sound of the bustling trees. She didn't like the silence. It was all she got when she sat in that room. If she was outside, she wanted conversation. "Where are we?"

"You know I'm not going to answer that."

She wrapped her arms around her legs, bringing them in for more comfort, "there are no fields like this in London."

"You're right."

Adara blinked, swivelling her head in his direction with a thumping sensation of detachment forming in her chest, "have you been outside London many times?" She shivered and then nodded. "Outside the country?" She nodded again, with her eyes boring into him.

She gulped and then took a swig of autumn air into her lungs, wondering how far she could push this interrogation: "You?"

He nodded slowly, stroking his black curtains back from the top of his eyes, "outside London, yeah. Never outside the UK."

She could feel the aura of longing radiating from the slow formation of his answer. She pressed further, "where do you want to go?"

He leant his back against the tree and rubbed his hair back again. "Spain."

She bit her lip, hoping she wasn't going to step outside of his boundaries, "why Spain?"

A few seconds passed and his sight remained fixed on the fields in front of him, before he began ripping at the grass. Adara dropped her head down and sighed.

"It's where my Dad was from."

Her eyes fluttered up at him: "Was?" He nodded, with his eyes concentrating on the grass.

She bit her lip and took another gulp of the crisp air, which was stroking her dry cheeks. Her large, grey eyes swept across the view in front of her before she sprang her head in his direction with a wide smile. "I've been to Spain. It's beautiful." He struck a small smile. "I spent a month out there with my friends. I figured out all the wonderful places to go and found so many lovely people."

Erikh fiddled with the chain around his neck with a hint of a smile, "I bet you did." Adara wrapped her arms around herself tighter, blinking in confusion. Erikh laughed, shaking his head and Adara's eyes widened, watching him whilst her stomach fluttered. No matter how old his journey made him appear, underneath all his protective layers he was still young, and she smiled in awe of his strength. She wanted to know his journey, and what made the lock on the gate of this prison more secure for him than it was for her.

She sat with her legs crossed, on a bench, wrapping her arms around her. The skies were grey, and the grass was wet, nevertheless, the fresh scent only called to her to stay longer. The field in front of her was empty and the rustling in the trees slowed her thoughts. She closed her eyes, listening to the heavy winds and she took a deep breath. The hairs standing on her skin were a sign that she could possibly become ill; she didn't care, the park gave her peace.

"It's calming isn't it." She jumped up onto her toes, trying to regain her balance. She saw Nayla hovering above the bench in her glowing form. She rolled her eyes. Nayla had been following her around for the past few days, trying to regain her forgiveness. Robyn couldn't lie, she was becoming used to this kinder form of her mother. However, the idea of handing over her trust so quickly was something that scared her.

"It was, yes, before you came along." Robyn would've walked off, but instead she decided to sit back down.

"So, are you going to go tomorrow?" Robyn bit her lip. Clare had told Robyn about Kris having a get together that she was keen on her going to. She was unsure if she would be welcome; not many of Tim's family seemed to be a fan of her. This didn't bother her; it was their reactions to her appearance that did. She didn't want to make things more difficult for Clare, especially after all the support she was giving her. Clare was also keen on her making amends with her sister. "Maybe it's a chance for you to open up to everyone a little." Robyn crinkled her eyebrows and focused on Nayla, with her jaw clenched slightly. "Baby steps."

"Yes, you would know about making amends and taking baby steps."

Nayla interlocked her hands together and swayed closer to Robyn, "don't make this about me Robyn, this is about you and your sister."

Robyn breathed deeply, "but don't you see, this *is* about you. This has all stemmed from you."

Nayla clicked her tongue, "No. I may have caused this," she nodded her head, "but you control the intentions for the outcome."

Robyn glanced at her mother again, with her teeth clenched, "I know it's easier said than done Robyn, but how you choose to move on with all the pain I've caused you is *your* choice. You've done amazingly well so far. You built your own foundations and surrounded yourself with someone that supported you. Keep doing that."

Robyn didn't want to hear this. She picked herself up from the bench. "Robyn, please give Estella a chance."

Robyn pulled at her hair, then spun around at her mother, "you both broke me!" Nayla hovered off the bench to place herself in front of Robyn, "do you understand that?!" Nayla nodded with her mouth open, "you kicked me out!" Nayla's head dropped, "do you realise the state that I was left in? The situations I found myself in?"

"Forgot about me, Robyn. Look how far you've come. All by yourself!" Robyn placed her palms on her temple, "please don't hold onto the past the way I did, because that will only hurt you more! The way I hurt myself through hurting you!" Robyn tried to concentrate on the rustling trees. "Estella was only young. She was just copying what I did, Robyn. Please don't take this out on her." Robyn lifted her brown eyes at the mother whose love she was so desperate to have during her adolescent life. Her jaw quivered as she accepted the tears dropping from her eyes.

Tuesday 10th April 2012

Kris sat smiling, noticing Reva talking to Robyn. Robyn's tender features were exploring Reva's mirroring of her words. He hadn't seen Robyn so lost in conversation with another person. He then realised it wasn't just any person. It was Reva. She had the ability to bring out the parts in people that they didn't know existed. She had the skill to make anyone feel comfortable, no matter where in the world they were. The thought of anyone putting her down when she had this in her fired him up like a match. It was Reva's light that made him not want to walk away from Adara. If Reva had it in her, he knew Adara had it in her somewhere too.

As he watched Robyn and Reva, Lauren appeared in front of him and placed herself on the arm of his chair. He shook his head when he saw her rainbow-coloured furry jumper and she grinned. He raised his eyes up at her and then to Clare before turning back to her. She shrugged, "you seemed too chicken, so I thought I'd do it for you." He sighed, knowing that she was trying to help him. Lauren rubbed her hands together and then tugged at the sleeves of her arm. "I'm going to go out with my mum soon." He gave her an encouraging smile, "I rang her, but she said that we should go out and... yeah. I told her I'll get back to her with a date." Kris squeezed her hand. "... and there's something else," she said.

Kris stared at her, waiting for her to continue. She whizzed her eyes around the room and began rubbing her hands again, "I found a new job." His eyes flew open. He moved forward on the sofa, ready to protest. Lauren waved her hands in a zigzag to hush him. He breathed in, readying himself for her explanation, "Kris, you're my best friend and it's really hard to find the right line with a best friend that's your boss." Lauren eyed him, "people talk in the office, Kris."

Kris's eyes broaden again before he tilted his head and blinked. He suddenly felt like he was in high school, being gossiped about for something he didn't do. He didn't realise their closeness was something to be interrogated, because there wasn't anything to be questioned. His shoulders dropped, "you're leaving because of these rumours?"

Lauren's hands waved and tutted, "No. No. I'm not leaving because of the rumours." She smiled at him, "I've been there for quite a few years now." Lauren raised her hands again, shushing his interruption, "I'm not leaving because of you. I'm leaving because I'm finding it too comfortable and because of that, people are talking. There's comfortable and then there's just *too* comfortable."

Lauren studied his expression whilst he rubbed the back of his neck. "Where's the new job?"

Lauren tugged at her sleeves again. Her lips formed a smile from ear to ear, "so..." Kris squinted watching her curiosity, "I've always been interested in like, beauty and nails and hair. I've always wanted to open up my own place and originally that's what I was saving for. I was always doing it on the side, until things went sideways literally. And now, although I haven't got that much savings, I've got just enough to invest in and a little bit more." Kris beamed, suddenly remembering her CV when she came to interview. It was littered with beauty courses and training on top of her other previous work experience. "I told Aunt Louise and she pushed me to rent this really, really small shop about twenty minutes from here..."

Kris suddenly felt something drop in him, "and I wouldn't have done?" Lauren's smile fell slightly, "Lauren, I can't put together one reason why you didn't tell me any of this. This stuff is amazing, and you think I wouldn't encourage you?"

Lauren chuckled lightly, "Kris I'm not putting you down or anything, but you hear of a venture and your fingers literally start twiddling like spiders. You're a complete control freak. If I did one thing wrong, you would want to fix the whole thing. I want to do this on my own." She tilted her head slightly, "maybe with help from you. But ninety five percent on my own." Kris opened his mouth again to interrupt, "...and on my terms!"

Kris nodded and then felt Lauren wrap her arms around him for a hug. She laughed until he finally hugged her back. He poured every unspoken thought into his hug. He'd never really expressed to her how thankful he was for her. "Lauren," he said when she let go of him, "you should've told me people talk."

She tilted her head, "Kris, people are going to no matter what you do. Don't worry so much. And, don't let it change your behaviour. They adore you the way you are, and they love being there the way it is." He nodded again and Lauren stared at him. "I'll go and get you a drink?"

As Lauren walked off, the doorbell rang, and he took a quick glance at the clock and saw Tim approach the door. Instantly, both Tim and Kris's jaws dropped. Kris met Clare's eyes from the other side of the room. He exhaled before storming into the kitchen, knowing Clare would follow him. He stopped at the counter and spun on his heel, "have you completely gone mad! Why are you bringing a load of drama here?"

Clare shook her head rapidly, "no drama Kris. I promise. No drama. They're going to go out for a walk and then they can do whatever they want. I promise. No drama!" He sighed, hearing the doorbell ring again. She shone her teeth at him and ran out of the kitchen to go and greet Estella.

He dropped his head in his hands and closed his eyes. "Party stress?" His head snapped up at the sound of that silken voice. His mouth went dry, allowing his eyes to travel over her. She was still tall even when wearing flats for driving. Her hair was in a low ponytail today. Her black stone ring hung on her neck by a silver chain over her long, black top. He took a deep breath, knowing it was that ring that was the massive rock between them. She kept her hands in the pockets of her trousers. He swallowed, trying to bring himself together to form words.

"You've got a nice house." He nodded, biting the bottom of his lips and realising that he was lost for the words that wouldn't lead to her suddenly transforming into a crazy cat. "Thank you for taking care of Reva."

"I told you. The workplace likes having her around." Adara smiled and he hoped it stayed that way. "How was work?"

"The usual. I'm starting to realise that I'm a bit tired of this place. They know I need the hours, so they take advantage."

Kris nodded and took in a deep breath. He put his hands into his pockets, "well, I'm always here to help out with Reva, so let me know if there's anything I can do." She stepped back and moved towards the door. His mouth went dry again, "stay for a while." Adara pocketed her hands, biting her bottom lip and Kris tried not to stare at her, "there's actually something I wanted to talk to you about." She blinked at him, waiting for him to continue. "It's none of my business…"

"If it's none of your business then I suggest you don't say anything," she warned with a bittersweet tone.

Kris scrutinised her, making sure not show how his chest twisted at the threat in her words. As she stepped back to turn, he blurted out, "you know Reva's being picked on in school, right?" Kris watched her go completely still and saw the spark in her round grey eyes fade. Before he could say anything further, she walked out of the kitchen.

Kris swung his head back, letting his leg hit the cupboard behind him. Lauren walked in with his drink and handed it to him, "the more I try to lessen the drama in my life, the more it just comes back."

"Yeah well, the way I see it is, you only take the drama because you choose to, you are always allowed to walk away." Kris sighed deeply before taking a big gulp of his brandy. "By the way, do you know Robyn's sister's here?"

"Yes, apparently my house has turned into a bloody therapy centre."

FRIDAY 30TH SEPTEMBER 1994

Though Erikh would still come and give her food and fresh clothes, she had pushed him away by trying to get closer to him. Malum had been away for a while. He was meant to be gone for a week, but it had been longer and she thought this would make her feel a little more at ease, however she felt as lonely as ever.

Something had happened. It came as no surprise to her that no-one was telling her anything. She had learnt something though. Her father was involved. Vidia hinted that her father didn't want her anymore. This wasn't true; her family loved her. She wasn't going to let a bunch of low-life strangers manipulate her into thinking any differently.

Adara was beginning to lose hope; she struggled to find ways to escape. The best plan she mustered was pretending to have a bath whilst leaving the water running, so that she could try to squeeze her way through the very small, thin window. There were too many flaws there. The window was too small. It would take too much time and they only gave her ten minutes to bathe. Then there were too many fields, where could she go?

The door opened, and her head swung up in the hopes of seeing Bane. Her lips dropped. Adara got up and stood near the lamp she had unplugged. She stood against the wall and watched her:

"Sweetcakes, chill out, I'm not here to hurt you." Vidia stepped in front of Adara to stroke her face. Adara shifted her face to the side and swallowed. "It's a shame: such a pretty girl and so unwanted." Adara froze, noticing Vidia playing with her hair by lightly tugging at it. She recoiled, feeling Vidia's mouth against her hair, "your Daddy thought his money was more important than you."

Adara tried shaking her head, but instead her legs began trembling. Her face became wet from Vidia's tongue against the skin near her ear. She attempted to reach out for the lamp. She heard the door screech open and Vida stepped back and smirked, "thought I'd cheer up our little friend." Erikh rolled his eyes. Vidia responded with a thin smile and walked out.

Adara stood on the spot, swallowing back the sandwich she had eaten earlier. Erikh's eyes focused on her taking a deep breath. Her hand was still outstretched, "you should've actually used the lamp."

Adara's shuddering legs found their way to the bed to sit down, "is she telling the truth?" Erikh nodded and bit his lip, approaching the bed to sit down next to her. She hid her face, with tears dribbling down her cheeks. She wrapped her legs around each other to stop them from shaking, "the rest of my family?"

"They're still looking for you." Adara wiped her face with the back of her sleeve, "your dad and Malum tried to start up a company a few years ago to make some money. Things went sideways from the start and the moment your dad got the sense that things weren't working, he took all the money, including Malum's, and ran for it. I think this was in Europe somewhere. Malum's been after your dad's blood and his money for a while. You have no idea how much your dad took from him. Anyway, Malum finally found out that you were all grown up and stubborn and took advantage of that. Malum assumed that your dad would show himself after he sent a letter to him about why you're missing, but your dad made no show of communication. A few days after Malum sent the letter, your dad disappeared. We don't even think he's in the UK anymore. Malum has gone to search for him, but I don't think it's going very well." Adara felt like she'd just been thrown in a deep, black well. During her childhood, whenever she wanted something, it wasn't her mother she would turn to; she was her father's daughter. She was the daughter of a man that would never let anything harm her. This man wasn't just her father, he was her *Dad*. A Dad that favoured her amongst his three children. She placed her hands over her face to stop the tears from releasing. She didn't want to cry for someone that had no love for her. "My mother did something similar to me when I was a child. It's how I ended up here."

Adara removed her hands from her face and tilted her head slightly, avoiding Erikh's gaze. He was looking at the walls and fiddling with the ring on his hand when he spoke, "my dad was killed when I was a child. After that, Mum was always high, angry and moving from man to man until she married one of them." He dropped his head slightly, "he moved us into his massive house. The husband gave me my own room, which he would come into and beat the crap out of me in whenever he was off his head." Adara gazed at him fiddling with his ring. "I eventually met Malum, who forced me to grow a pair and stand up for myself. So, I told my Mum to either choose me or the alcoholic rich husband." Erikh tilted his head towards Adara, "Malum took me in, gave me a home and in return I do whatever he wants. The people here have accepted me. If I walk away, no-one will want to know me."

Adara tilted her head in his direction, searing her eyes into him, "that's not true. If people met the person I know, then they would want to know you." They both sat quietly in each other's silence. Adara was still thinking of her father, trying to recover from the sickness of a darkening state of rejection. She touched the side of her face, which was still trickling from Vida's tongue. "What's going to happen to me?"

Erikh bit his bottom lip, shaking his head. He got off the bed and left the room, leaving her with only her tears for company.

Tuesday 10th April 2012

Robyn was trying to stay calm amongst the amount of people in the room. The noises were flooding her brain and there were too many voices. The only one that kept her breathing for some reason, was the little girl Reva, who had been sitting talking to her most of the time. She was a sweet little girl with a brilliant, melodious voice. She kept talking to her about little things. Marbles. People. Water. Trees. Televisions. Food. Pictures. Colours. The random topics kept Robyn distracted. Now, ever since Reva's mother had come to take her, she had to face the reality in front of her. Estella was now in the house with her.

If it wasn't for her mother's voice continuously telling her to trust Clare, she would've left. Clare had come over to her place a few days after her mother had appeared. Every time her mother would appear and leave, it made her feel like her presence only occurred in her mind. Robyn was beginning to get used to the chill that she left behind; to the point it still lingered on her skin. Her head still tingled too, from the way her mother would now stroke her head until she'd fall asleep.

After a while, Estella came to sit down next to her. "You okay?" she asked. Robyn nodded slowly, trying to keep a smile on her face. Estella gazed around the room. "This is an amazing house, isn't it?" Robyn moved her head up and down whilst running her eyes over her sister, who was wearing simple jeans and a thin, black jumper for the unusual weather. Her blue boots stretched up to her knees and her hair was tied back in a messy pony like she'd tied it up in a rush.

Clare approached them, smiling, "Why don't the both of you go out in the garden? I think Robyn finds the noise annoying."

Estella jumped up with a smile, "or we could go for a walk?" Robyn glanced at the floor, then felt a light whisper in her ears. The crisp air was a reminder of her mother's presence. She got up, nodding her head, unable to let any words leave her mouth.

Robyn and Estella made their way out of the door. Robyn felt the cool air hit her and she wanted nothing more than to experience more of the cold, rather than heat. It made her eyes see more clearly and the threads in her mind reattach one by one. "How do you know the person that lives here?"

"He's my ex-boyfriend's cousin," Robyn said, breathing in the air that was untangling bits of her thoughts.

The streetlamps lit the way for them to walk whilst Estella's heels tapped the dry ground beneath them. "Robyn, I was a really stupid teenager and I get that you're going to be angry and it will take time some time to forgive me but…" Estella stopped in her tracks, "maybe we don't start with forgiveness. Maybe we don't even start as sisters. Maybe we just start as acquaintances. Start at the beginning and try to build a friendship and see where that takes us."

Robyn glanced at her sister, not knowing what to say. There was a black fear looming around her, the desire for a positive change overrode this. Maybe this was it. Her mother was talking about doors and how they would lead to new paths. Maybe this was a door that she had to be willing to open, no matter how much she wanted to leave it locked. She looked down at her hands with a deep exhale. For once, she wanted to be able to heed a mother's advice, even if it was a mother that was cruel to her throughout her adolescence. "He left me."

Estella nodded with understanding, "my ex left me too. I couldn't commit. Maybe it's to open a space for us in each other's lives. And who knows? Maybe that may lead to finding someone else? And this time we'll be stronger in the relationship, because we've got each other."

Robyn stared down at the street ahead of her, "not really much of a walk is it?"

Estella's smile broadened while her large eyes journeyed up, her lashes fluttering, "not really," her long thin finger pointed upwards, "but at least we get to see some stars. We don't get that a lot in London." London had brought unusual weather today. It wasn't so warm, so only a thin jacket was needed to protect her skin from the tender chill. The long line of spectacular Georgian houses were standing out beneath a blanket of little diamonds that London's sky had decided to amaze them with this evening. Robyn's eyes opened wider, realising how thankful she was for the breathtaking view. The plush houses made her feel like she had just landed in a period film. The beam of the streetlamp in front of her was made redundant, because the sparkling skies lit up the houses, making them seem even grander.

She blinked at them in awe, before turning back to Estella. "Do you work?"

Estella nodded, bringing her head down, "yeah, I'm a waitress. I didn't have the patience for anything, so I went from job to job not building any career. I've been hunting for a new job for ages! It's hard." Robyn stared at the floor, biting her lip and scratching her head before turning on her heel to walk ahead; Estella joined in unison, "what happened when you went off on your own?" She asked. Robyn focused on the tall houses in front of her, trying not to think of the situations she ended up in or the people that she had encountered. Estella suddenly stopped again and wrapped her arms around Robyn, making her freeze. She didn't want to be stiff, the act of letting go was new to her though. Robyn hadn't been hugged by anyone other than Tim in so long. Even when his mother hugged her, she didn't know how to react. She heard her sister's scattered breathing and sniffing. Robyn gradually allowed her hands to rest on her sister's back. She took a heavy sigh, knowing that this hug was filling in the missing time that they should've spent together. Estella held onto her until her phone rang.

Robyn wiped her face and listened to her sister talk to Clare and then put the phone down. "Shall we go somewhere by ourselves to eat? It'll give us more time to talk rather than impose on their thing."

Robyn glimpsed both ends of the street before she felt a chill trace across the back of her hand. She focused her concentration on her fingers and then at her sister, bringing a small smile to her face. "For now, let's continue imposing. I owe Clare that, after everything she's done for me."

"Is your ex the one that came to see me?"

Robyn clicked her tongue, "no, that's his cousin Kris. This is his house."

Estella nodded then grinned. "Is the brown-haired girl his girlfriend?" Robyn squinted. "He's cute." Estella hopped in her walk a little and Robyn bit her lip, containing a giggle.

Robyn narrowed her eyes, exploring her sister's face, "I don't think Kris is interested in a relationship Estella. From what I know anyway. He lost his wife." Estella shrugged her shoulders, grinning widely and watching Robyn ring the doorbell. "How about we concentrate on us for a while and then guys later?"

Estella tilted her head to the side and pouted with her nude-coloured lips. "I think we can do both, we're women after all!" Robyn moved her head side to side until Kris opened the door. Estella's large eyes shot wide open, travelling back to Robyn, who laughed.

Robyn saw Kris's owl eyes boring into her with his mouth agape, "can we come in?"

Kris blinked and then nodded before standing aside. He placed his hand out, "I'm Kris, by the way, we met before at the restaurant."

Estella grinned and bit her tongue, "yes," she nodded slowly, "I most definitely remember." Kris blinked again at their hands. Robyn cleared her throat loudly and Estella brought her hand back.

"Umm," Kris pointed ahead towards the large family room, "make yourselves comfortable," he said, walking towards the kitchen.

Estella walked on ahead and Robyn took a deep breath, with her gaze lingering on the kitchen. She focused at the floor, scratching her head. She knew what she wanted to do, she just didn't know how. Her hair waved slightly, and she picked up her head, whizzing her eyes around until they stopped at a glowing Nayla floating next to the staircase.

"What's stopping you?" Robyn blinked at the floor. "You're only trying to help her..." Robyn bit her lip, "and you'll be helping yourself too." She lifted her head up towards her mother. "You'll feel good about yourself for asking. What's the worst that could happen? The worst has already happened, there's nothing you have left to be afraid of." Robyn stared at Nayla with her brown eyes wide open. She nodded, before making her way towards the kitchen.

She rubbed her hands together and pushed her feet forward, feeling completely out of her own skin. Kris spun around, hearing the sound of her footsteps. "Sorry. Just wanted to ask you something." His features softened before leaning back against the counter to give her his full attention. "I know Tim hasn't probably portrayed a great picture of me, and frankly I don't really blame him..."

"I don't think you should blame yourself either." Robyn stared at him, then redirected her eye contact towards the ground.

She swallowed and held onto her sleeves, "I don't really know why I'm doing this. Maybe Clare has got into my head faster than I'd thought." Kris smiled and Robyn cleared her throat, knowing his eyes were on her, "Estella said she's been looking for a new job for a while and I was hoping you could help her out."

Kris nodded again, "I'll give her a call."

Robyn breathed and let go of her sleeves, "thanks."

She was about to turn to make her way out the kitchen, when Kris called to her, "Robyn?" She looked back at him. "I hope you don't mind my saying, but you should laugh more often. It suits you." Robyn bit her bottom lip remembering the way she was laughing when Estella and she were at his front door.

FRIDAY 7TH SEPTEMBER 2012

The morning light beamed through his window, waking him up. He pulled the blanket over his head, shielding his eyes from the light. He wasn't ready to get up yet: he closed his eyes until sleep found him again. A little while later, he heard it again. The sound of his name came softly, and he tugged at his blanket. She whispered his name again and he tutted underneath the covers.

The blanket slowly lifted, and he felt a cold breeze flicker through his hair. He dragged the blanket back up, only for it to be blown back. He bolted up. His eyes grew and he felt something drop inside of him.

She was wearing a long, white dress that waved slightly in the wind. Her long, brown locks swung around her round face in the breeze and her soft lashes fluttered, making the strength in her green eyes delicate. She wasn't a ghost. The glimmer in her skin told him she wasn't a ghost. He budged forward slightly, breathing in deeply enough to take in the warmth of her small hands in his.

He blinked at his surroundings. The long river of water rushed ahead into the trees and the leaves bustled through the chilly wind. He brought his eyes back to her again to see her drop her head, "what do you want me to do?"

"Stop thinking so much," Kelci answered, waving her hand at her surroundings, "it won't help you move on. Look at what's in front of you and appreciate it." Kris rubbed his hands through his hair, breathing deeply. Kelci tilted her head, "make something new."

Kris shook his head before resting his eyes on the water in front of him, "I don't want new." Kris explored the way in which she played with her fingers. He squinted his eyes in thought at his book: "it was you."

She nodded her head, "I told you, I'll always be with you."

Kelci kept her head down, fiddling with her fingers. He closed his eyes, "if it were the other way around, would you want me to be saying this to you?" He opened his eyes and directed them at the rushing water that disappeared behind the branches and leaves, "would you want to forget everything?" Kris brought his eyes back to her and an anchor dropped inside him. Kelci was staring at her knees as streams of tears were running down her cheeks. He shifted himself forward to wipe her tears and to rest his forehead against hers before closing his eyes.

Out of nowhere, he felt something heavy tug at him from the back and his arms flew upwards. He stopped breathing until he fell with a thud onto his bed. His eyes bolted open and he sprang up from his bed, seeing his window wide open.

His eyes scanned his room before he placed his head down in between his knees, pacing his breathing. Kelci appeared in the forefront of his mind. It wasn't a dream.

His eyes snapped back open at hearing his phone ring and he checked the time before running downstairs. Lauren walked in with a frown. He assumed it was from the six missed calls he'd given her. She stomped into his kitchen to make them both a cup of coffee, "you know Lauren, I'm beginning to wonder whether to just give you a key." Lauren poured milk into her coffee, "I thought you were done with the early morning matchmaking." She nodded her head. "Why are you here then?" Lauren placed her hand on her hip. "In that really hideous top." She was wearing a bright orange top with massive holes and white dots of cotton. "I hope you're not wearing that to work." Lauren tilted her head whilst handing him his coffee. "Lauren, talk. My mindreading skills are lacking this morning."

She slammed her mug down on the cream-coloured counter. "You promised you'd help me with my plans for the salon! You took the day off to help me and everything."

Kris blinked, checking his mobile calendar. He closed his eyes and nodded. "Sorry."

Lauren squinted her eyes at him. "You're a little all over the place these days, aren't you?"

"There's actually a few things I wanted to say to you about your salon." Lauren took out her notepad. "So, basically, Robyn spoke to me." Lauren lifted her eyes and scooted in her seat to speak. Kris shot his eyes at her and she pretended to zip her lips. "She told me that her sister wants a new job, so I was thinking maybe you could take a look at her CV, see what she's done before and maybe think of hiring her as a trainee? Maybe get some courses and put her in training?" Kris raised his hand to stop her from interrupting, "also, Adara is after a new job and she is loaded with experience." Kris picked up his mug and sipped. The heat that rushed down helped to wake him up a little.

"Okay, so just to confirm and reiterate, you want me to hire your stroppy girlfriend and Tim's strange ex-girlfriend's sister? Is that correct?"

Kris rolled his eyes, "if I judged every single person that walked into my workplace, I'd have no employees. It's their work ethic that counts."

Lauren huffed, "how the hell can I afford courses and to hire people like Adara!"

"We'll find funding for courses and one proper, experienced employee isn't going to be that expensive, Lauren. You need someone with real experience to keep the customers reassured that your employees know what they're doing." Lauren gritted her teeth. "Any other problems?" Kris asked.

"No, but I do have a question." Kris glanced at her over his mug. "What's happening with Adara? I haven't seen her around lately. And I know you miss Reva." She pouted, "and Ayva says everyone misses her at the office."

Kris's eyes travelled down to his mug. "She hasn't been around lately because nothing's happening."

Lauren tilted her head, "is that why you didn't say anything to me when I called her your stroppy girlfriend?" Kris rolled his eyes, not wanting to further the conversation. He hadn't seen Adara and Reva in weeks and he did miss them. It seemed that

Adara had stopped Reva from running to his office after she had done so a couple of times at the beginning of her summer holidays. Adara ignored the two texts he'd sent to sort out whatever the issue was. Her dismissal made him give up. He didn't like being pushed back and he couldn't be bothered with anyone's crazy secrets and dramas. He'd experienced all that he could, and he didn't want to take on anymore. Adara had built this great wall around them, so he couldn't even help Reva, who he was worried about.

When he put his head up to look at Lauren, he jumped back with his eyes wide open, spilling all his coffee.

Lauren sprinted her way around to him. He stood watching Kelci on the other side of the kitchen. Her full lips beamed at him in her ghostly form before fading. He took in a deep breath and grabbed hold of the edge of the counter to lower his head and pace his breathing. He felt Lauren's hand on his shoulder. He blinked his eyes gathering his strength to pull himself up straight, "Kris, remember we said talking helps?"

Kris eyed Lauren, noticing her eyes analysing him. He took in a deep breath, "promise you won't think I'm crazy, or that I'm losing it or something? Or that," he put his fingers up in quotation marks, "I'm becoming a sad old man?" Lauren squinted at him. "I keep having dreams of Kelci and I keep seeing and hearing her everywhere." Lauren placed herself back down on the kitchen chair with her eyebrows raised. Kris began nodding his head rapidly, "you think I'm going crazy." He began wiping the kitchen counter, "just forget it."

"I didn't say that." Kris stopped wiping. "I think that you've got a lot going on and subconsciously you're confused, because this is the first woman you may really like since Kelci."

Kris rolled his eyes, "I don't need to hear this." He placed his palms on the counter, "all this deep stuff."

Lauren tugged at her sleeves, "Kris, you're hearing and probably seeing your dead wife. I think that's as deep as it gets." Kris shot his eyes at her. "Look, go upstairs, get some rest. I'll come back at ten to work on my plans with you. If you want to talk about it then, we can. If you don't, then that's fine too. But, I do think that if what you're saying is true, then she's trying to tell you something."

Kris pulled at his hair, "but what?" he dropped his hands, "what is she trying to tell me?"

Lauren tilted her head at him to smile slightly.

Saturday 5th November 1994

Since their conversation, a few weeks had passed. Erikh would just come into her room twice a day and leave her clothes and a sandwich with a large bottle of water. Up until this point, she was still crying herself to sleep and hoping her life would play out like some of the animated films her friends forced her to watch. Those films were now the things giving her any inkling of hope. If it wasn't for the replayed thoughts of a prince climbing through a window, then she would've completely lost her sense of sanity by now.

When she was bored, she would sit by the door on the other side of the room and try to hear snippets of their conversations. They were worried. Malum was still missing and they had no idea what to do with her. Adara took in the grassy fields outside her window in wonder. If he was gone, Adara was happy; she now had some solid hope.

"Happy Birthday," she lifted her head, seeing Vidia standing halfway across the room with her hand on her hip and a pink cupcake in the other hand. Adara was sitting on the floor against her bed. This was her room now. She got up from the floor and made her way towards the unplugged lamp. Vidia brought herself closer to Adara, waving the cupcake in her hand, "you don't want your birthday cake? I went to the shops especially for you and everything." Adara ignored her question, ensuring she kept her hand near the lamp. "I'm excited." She shrugged her shoulders with a big smile. "Malum's going to be back soon." Vidia stuffed her finger deep into the cupcake, pulled it out and licked the contents off.

"Maybe you should share the cupcake with him." Adara said. Vidia smirked and scraped the icing off her cupcake with her long nail.

"Look who found her tongue." Vidia placed the icing on the tip of her tongue. She stepped closer, placing herself directly in front of Adara, making Adara inhale deeply.

"I never lost it." Vidia tilted her neck, ready to respond when the door screeched open behind them. She simpered before planting the cupcake down near the lamp. Erikh held the door open for her. Vidia strolled out, swinging her long plait from side to side. Adara remained frozen in place by the lamp, noticing Erikh approach her with his eyes on the ground. He picked up the cupcake and left the room.

The length his hair had grown for her marked how long she'd been stuck in the room. She hadn't even realised it was her birthday.

Friday 18th June 1992

"Dad, can we have pizza today?" Adara heard her brother plead with their Dad. She kept her head stuck in her maths book, however she noticed her Dad ignore her brother. He had one hand in his pocket and a notepad in the other hand that demanded his attention. Her father then walked out of the room, still wearing his long grey jacket, informing her he wasn't going to be home that long.

"Adara?" She tilted her face slightly. Her brother's round face grinned at her, "are you hungry?" She rolled her eyes, throwing her pen down on her book. She knocked before walking straight into her father's bedroom. She gasped, taking in the scattered notes of money laying all over the bed.

"Adara, next time you wait for me to tell you to come in." Her eyes scanned the bed before nodding. "What is it?" He asked.

Her pillowy thick lips formed a smile, "pizza."

Her father scooped up a few notes from the bed and handed it to her. She pointed at the bed. Her father placed his finger over his mouth, "shush."

Friday 7th September 2012

Kris had spent the last few hours working endlessly with Lauren on her plans. She didn't raise the subject of Kelci with him and he appreciated that. He knew Kelci wanted him to move on and he was trying. If only she could see that.

Lauren's ideas were perfect and on point. She had saved the right amount of money and should have good results. She had written out a well thought out plan of her concepts, actions, ideas to implement, competitive markets, consumers and team.

Kris now left her in his dining room whilst he sat in his car outside Reva's school. He didn't have a clue what he was doing. All he could think was that Kelci wanted him to try harder, so he was going to try and speak to Adara face to face. He got out of the car and took a deep breath. Adara stood next to the school gate in a different beige-coloured coat to the one he'd seen before. Her long, black hair hung loose by her arms and she was wearing high-heeled boots. She had walked to the school. Her eyes lifted from her mobile and sprung open when she saw him. She marched up to him and he leaned his back against the car, ready for her to argue with him.

"What are you doing here?" He forgot how airy her voice was, like a kite. Kris rubbed the base of his neck, trying to find words. Adara shook her head, "Kris, you haven't contacted me in months." Kris pulled himself up from the car and stood facing her, "and now you're here outside the school?"

He blinked, "Adara I texted twice, and I've come here because you didn't respond. I didn't…" Adara glanced over her shoulders and he closed his eyes, "is Reva okay?"

Adara rolled her eyes, "texting someone twice within the space of three months doesn't count." Kris's eyes grew, noticing Adara glance over her shoulder again, "look, parents around here are a bit weird. They'll…"

He rubbed his jaw and scoffed, "you didn't respond to me when I told you your child's picked on in school but you're worried about gossipy people that obviously have nothing better to do than talk about things that have nothing to do with them?" Adara's eyes sparked and he realised he'd hit a nerve. A smile sprang to his lips upon seeing Reva running at them with her arms open.

Reva flung her arms around him. "Kris! How come you're here?" He couldn't believe that she had grown slightly taller in the few months he hadn't seen her.

"I missed you so much, that's why." Reva let go of him and she showed him her dimples with her brown eyes lit up. "I'll drop you back home." Adara opened her mouth to object. He shot his eyes at her, "you're going to refuse a free lift?"

The drive was silent for the first few minutes and he could see in the mirror that Reva's head was switching from her mother and him, hoping for one of them to talk. "It's my birthday tomorrow Kris!" Kris grinned broadly. "It's Saturday tomorrow and Mum's working. She's leaving me with my friend's mother."

"Is this the same mother that didn't bother keeping an eye on you whilst you ran all the way to my office in deep snow?"

Adara rolled her eyes, "no, it isn't." Kris noticed her fiddling with the black stone ring around her neck.

Reva dropped her head and scooted back in her seat. She lifted her head at the mirror again, "are you working tomorrow?" Kris shook his head. "Could we go to the movies?" Adara, kept her eyes on the muggy, car-clustered road ahead. He smiled lightly at Reva from his mirror, witnessing the absence of twinkle in her eyes. She dropped her head again, pulling at the string on her school bag. The rest of the drive was filled with the sound of cars rushing past them before they reached Adara's house.

Kris parked the car in Adara's spotless driveway and Reva immediately ran out. Adara's hand moved to the door, "Adara." She lifted her eyes to see Reva walk into the house and then brought her hand back. Her eyes were dimmed, similar to the way stars may lose their sparkle. He sighed and rubbed his head, "Adara, tell me, did I get this whole thing wrong? You talk to me like you want me to stay and then you shut me out, but let Reva see me, and then when I try to help, you slam the door in my face." Kris resisted from turning to look at her. "I came today because it's not only Reva that I miss. But if you really don't want me around, then say it, and I won't interfere with you and Reva at all." Kris concentrated on his steering wheel, though he could see her staring at him from the corner of his eyes, "but if you want me to stick around, then this massive hole you made between us needs to go, because I'm completely falling in it right now. You need to be open and real with me." Kris glanced at her and his eyelids shot up when he saw that Adara's charcoal eyes were bright red, like they'd just been set on fire.

Monday 7th November 1994

She felt her shoulder shake. She refused to face the boring reality of the cream room around her. She felt a big jolt at the side of her shoulder that forced her eyelids open. She didn't have time to process what was happening. Erikh just threw the blanket off of her and dragged her out of the bed. She tried to speak whilst she was being hurled to the door that she'd never dared to open over the year. Erikh stopped at the door. "Just stay quiet. Understood?" She stared into his patchy-brown eyes, "just nod." She swallowed and then took a deep breath in before nodding. Erikh opened the door and the vision in front of her appeared like a desert. The walls, the marble and the furniture were sandy coloured with little freckles of black dots. The building wasn't what she expected. She was waiting to see other rooms with door numbers and a desk, until she saw pictures on the wall of people she didn't recognise. She wanted to stop Erikh in his rushed tracks to investigate the house that had been holding her captive.

The high-pitched voice sent a shiver down her spine as rapidly as it made Erikh stall in his tracks. "So soon pet? You didn't even say bye bye." Her breathing staggered. Vidia stood at the doorway of one of the rooms with her hands folded. Erikh let go of Adara's hand. She couldn't comprehend his expression when he glanced at her, then whizzed his eyes to Vidia. She rotated her hand in a circle, gesturing at her surroundings. "I get why you want to go, Erikh." Vidia glared at him. His chest raised when he exhaled deeply. Adara's eyes explored Erikh; she had never seen this expression on him, and it confused her. Vidia stepped out of the doorway and stood in front of him, "you should leave the brat though. It's like you said; Malum would have his own plans for her."

The moment Vidia's hand reached for Adara, Erikh wrapped his hand around Vidia's neck and covered her mouth with his other hand before she could scream. He pushed her against the round table in the middle of the hallway. Adara's hand flew to her mouth to stop herself from screaming. Erikh squeezed Vidia's neck and Adara backed herself in the corner of the hallway. Vidia's hands were rubbing all over Erikh's face, trying to push him away before her body seeped down to the floor like unwanted silk. Erikh craned his neck, searching for her. She crept out of the corner and Erikh brought his hand out to her. Her sight lingered on Vidia's long figure sprawled on the sand-coloured marble. He followed her eyes. "She isn't dead." Erikh gradually moved closer to her and took her hand.

Erikh forced her eyes away from Vidia when he dragged her through the hallway. He swung open the front door and Adara let out a small shriek at the sight of Malum. His dark pupils flew between the two of them before travelling to the end of the hallway to see his girlfriend's resting body. His eyes popped into wide balls; he hissed, grabbing hold of Erikh's hair and hitting him against the wall. Adara's hand flew to her ears. She screamed, racing back down the hallway. She stopped at a cupboard that was underneath a long flight of stairs. She quickly opened it and scanned the contents of the long shelves. Her eyes stopped when they found the answer she needed.

With hope in her hands she ran back to Malum, who was sitting on Erikh with his legs on either side of him and his hands around his neck. Closing her eyes, she swung the metal bat over Malum's head and heard the crack of his skull that made her insides quiver. Her hands shuddered, releasing the bat, which echoed with a loud clang against the marble. Her eyes grew and she stepped back.

Malum's body fell on Erikh like a large bird and he quickly hauled it off of him. Blood coursed in all directions like an octopus's legs. Adara strode away from the mess before her and before she knew it, she kneeled to throw up. Her legs shivered before she felt the cold marble.

Tuesday 8th November 1994

Adara's eyes fluttered open, expecting to feel soft, warm blankets and see a cream wall in front of her. All she saw were metal shelves, all lined up with cans of paint. She sat up and the memories came flooding back to her. The metal bat. The crack. Blood. Fresh blood spilling everywhere. She curled into a ball. Closing her eyes, she swallowed and paced her breathing before getting up to open the door. She followed the route of the dark, narrow corridor. The tiles were off-white and black in between the gaps. She wrapped her arms around herself and her eyes sprang open when she felt a hand over her mouth. She was being dragged backwards.

She heard the door shut behind her and the hand come off of her mouth, "are you stupid? You don't go walking off like that by yourself. You wait for me to come back." She observed him, realising his clothes were different from what she remembered.

He gestured to something he was holding when her hands flew to her mouth. She couldn't contain the picture flickering through her mind. "I killed Malum."

Erikh shook his head, bringing her hands down with a sigh, "don't repeat that." He shoved the clothes towards her, "we need to keep moving Adara, put these on." She brought her hands back and eyed her surroundings, "this is my old workplace." Erikh took her hands and placed the clothes in them. Her nose flared at the ripped pair of black joggers and oversized hoodie. He rolled his eyes before walking out of the small box room.

∼

They'd been walking for a while now. Adara had no clue where they were; Erikh had instructed her to keep her head down whilst he pulled her through the streets. She would've thought that the whole time sitting in one room would've given her a lot of energy, however her body felt like she was pulling a building. The images of Malum's blood were still moving around in between her eyes and she could still smell the metallic rush of blood.

The only positivity she was gaining was the feel of the singing wind swishing against her skin and the smell of wet leaves lingering around her nose. She wanted to stop and take it all in. She hadn't felt so alive in such a long time. Though she appreciated the breaks in the field, walking on a pavement around other human beings and hearing the sound of cars zooming past was altogether a different sensation; a frenetic one.

Her legs gave way slightly when lowering one foot in front of another whilst Erikh gradually led her down a flight of stairs. He opened the door to a shed and he lightly pushed her inside by the shoulders. The smell of damp soil hit her. "Stay here. Don't leave here."

Her eyes widened and she felt the small walls of the dark shed close in on her. She grabbed his arm, "no." He blinked at her, "you can't leave me here!" Adara stared at him. A sharp pain entered her chest, making her lips quiver. She held onto his arm like a child. "Why can't I come with you?"

Erikh stepped inside the shed. He undid the sliver chain around his neck and then removed his black stone ring, "I'm worried someone is going to recognise you." He placed the ring on the chain and clipped it around her neck. "I'm not leaving you. I'll be back for this. Lock the door behind me. Hold on to this ring. Count really slow to two thousand. I'll knock three times in three sequences. That's when you open. Understood?" She suddenly felt like she was back in the room, waiting for Erikh to walk through the door. She inspected the shed. Other than the pots and plants, there was hardly anything in there with her. "Just nod."

Erikh squinted at her and softly grazed his lips on her head before leaving the shed. She breathed in the damp air then sat down on one of the pots. She rotated Erikh's ring around her fingers before eyeing it closely. The ring was thick, heavy silver and the design was worn. It must've been in Erikh's family for years. The large, black stone was encased with silver circles. She heard footsteps outside, and her breathing scattered. She tightened her grip on the ring and closed her eyes to begin counting.

The two thousand seconds had to be slowest time of her life before she jolted up from the door after three knocks, three times in a row. She opened the door and swung her arms around Erikh's neck, forcing him to stagger back. She heard a thud before he wrapped his arms around her. She felt his hand on her head when she rested her cheek against his chest. His heart was racing before it fell into a natural rhythm. She breathed slowly and they stood for a while before she glanced down beside his feet. She stared at the large bag he had come in with and then blinked up at him.

"Malum's brother and Vidia are now looking for us." She closed her eyes and gulped at the image of Malum's blood all over the marble, seared into the forefront of her mind. Erikh took Adara's arms from around his neck and placed a kiss on the inside of both her hands. "Did you mean it when you said you trusted me?" She studied his tired features and nodded.

Part Four

Tuesday 4th September 2012

"After a few months of hiding out, Erikh managed to get us out of the country."

Kris stared ahead through his car window and out at Adara's house. He could hear Adara breathing slowly next to him and he could hear all the questions jumping around in his mind. It was only the sound of the cars that reminded him everything was still moving, otherwise it all felt stagnant. He heard the pull of the door handle and knew she was leaving the car. He couldn't find the right words to stop her.

Only one thought reached his voice. He couldn't find it in him to look at her as he asked, "Reva?"

Adara stepped out, "is Erikh's."

After hearing the door shut, Kris reversed out of Adara's driveway without glancing back.

Was it even true? Was she telling a dramatic lie? None of what she said made sense. If this had happened to her, why did she not report it? Kris felt stupid for not asking any of these questions. Instead of making his way back home; he turned his car another direction. The day was becoming dark and the roads were busy; people were now making their way back from work. He took a long drive, hearing Adara's words play in his head. It had to be a massive lie. None of it could be real.

He stopped his car outside his restaurant and stared ahead at the bench where he had proposed to his wife. Life had been extremely confusing at that point, nevertheless everything still had a direction. He knew he wanted a career. He knew he wanted to make his mother happy and his Dad proud. He knew he wanted to make the Dauni business a large conglomerate. His priorities had changed since then. Kelci's passing changed all of this. If only he realised earlier that his priorities should change, maybe he wouldn't be in search of a direction now.

He needed advice. No matter what, he would always care for Reva; nonetheless, everything Adara had told him shifted his perspective.

∼

Aunt Louise's face lit up seeing him on her doorstep. He kissed his Aunt's cheek before he entered the house. He removed his coat and placed it in the cloakroom. He then followed the scent of the concoction that overtook his nose to find Chinese rice in the kitchen. "How have you been, Aunt Louise?"

"The usual, keeping myself busy. I managed to get myself a job as a receptionist in a sales company." Aunt Louise covered the food and he followed her into the living room.

"I didn't even know you were looking for a job," Kris said, before putting a spoon of stir fry in his mouth and chewing.

"Well, rent doesn't pay itself." Kris's eyes sprang open. He swallowed his food quickly, "you're renting this place?" Aunt Louise tilted her head; her red lips pursed at him, "didn't you get any money from the divorce?" Aunt Louise shrugged. "Aunt Louise, the money through the divorce is rightly yours just as it is his."

Aunt Louise tutted, "you may be right, but I don't want his money. I'm perfectly happy working for a roof over my head." Kris blinked. "Now, not that I'm complaining, but what's prompted your sudden visit?"

Kris placed his bowl down on the floor; Aunt Louise stared at him, waiting for him to talk. He took a deep breath and began retelling Adara's story. When he finished explaining every detail of what he'd been told, Aunt Louise's expression was mute. He watched her chew the inside of her mouth. The silence was making him feel on edge. "You're not giving any reaction." Aunt Louise got up to grab herself a furry brown blanket from the side of the sofa and then sat back down to wrap herself with it. "Aunt Louise, I've just told you that my friend was kidnapped when she was a child, you could at least be a little surprised!"

Aunt Louise shrugged, "you hear of these stories all the time. In the newspapers, on the news." She tilted her head with her eyebrows raised, "it could be anyone. What's her name?"

Kris leaned back into the sofa rubbing his hand through his hair, "Adara Fields."

"I remember just before Tim went to uni, Jack told me…", Kris tried not to grind his teeth, "…there was a kidnap story where it was rumoured that the father went missing after a while. The girl never came back, if I remember correctly. Or, maybe she did, and it was never publicised. I can't remember the girl's name though, it was a very long time ago. Do you have the father's name?" Kris shrugged. "Didn't you ask her?" Kris dropped his eyes, making his Aunt purse her lips, "you didn't just drive off?"

"I didn't know what to say!" Kris leaned in, "what was I supposed to do?"

Aunt Louise tucked herself further into the blanket. "I guess being told a story like that first-hand from the victim isn't exactly easy."

Kris rubbed the base of his neck, "what do you think I should do?"

Aunt Louise bored her brown eyes into him before shaking her head, "that's not for me to answer. You don't have to make a decision right away, but the longer you take making that decision the harder you'll find it to go back."

Kris gazed at the picture of Kelci and his mother that Aunt Louise placed over the shelf over her fireplace. Those days only seemed like they were yesterday; they were crystal clear in his mind. Kelci, his mother and Aunt Louise rented a cottage in the countryside for the week. He was annoyed that the three people he communicated with the most in his life had left him on his own. It was one of the most boring weeks of his life. It was during this time he really realised how much of an impact Kelci actually had on him. He had missed her so much in every way and he kept thinking to himself how much he never wanted to feel that way again.

"That was one of the best weeks ever. Kelci was over the moon to be getting out of the house."

Kris shook his head, then narrowed his eyes at his aunt, "you're talking as if I bolted her to the house."

"I never said you did but she did get bored at times."

Kris's eyes fixated back to Kelci's small smile. "She had every option to do whatever made her happy."

"As do you." Kris listened to his aunt, searching for an answer in her words, "but just remember Kris, whatever choice you make affects that little girl the most. She doesn't need any more confusion in her life. If you don't want to support her, then now is the time to walk away."

S ATURDAY 8TH S EPTEMBER 2012

Kris woke up the next morning, holding onto his head. He had spent the whole night working with Lauren on her plans. She was set and Kris was going to make sure her plans were successful.

Adara's story came flooding back to him when he unlocked his blackberry. He rubbed his head, then pulled himself out of bed to get ready for the day. Black trousers and a black jumper seemed casual enough for him.

An hour or so later, he was driving to Adara's house, until it dawned on him that she was at work. He parked up outside the house and texted Adara for Reva's location. The message came up as read immediately. He began tapping his steering wheel, whilst he waited for her response. He knew what she was thinking on the other end of the phone. He saw her typing and his finger began tapping the wheel harder.

After a few seconds, he sighed and began driving.

∽

Kris approached the stranger's house and rang the doorbell. It was an old, red-brick house.

A short lady opened the door, she introduced herself as Jodie in a high-pitched, energetic voice, saying ,"come inside." Kris could hear Reva shouting from somewhere in the small house. "So, have you known Adara long?"

"I guess." Jodie gave a perky grin and walked to the living room. Kris felt the warmth of the house. There were tones of the colour brown everywhere. The pictures on the wall all showed a young girl who he assumed was Reva's friend. The large television took over the space of the small living room and the sofas looked so inviting they made Kris want to lay down on them.

Reva ran into the room screaming his name, and he bent down, taking her into a big hug. "Happy Birthday!" A small girl with shoulder-length blonde hair watched them from behind her and he let go of Reva. She had the smallest button nose Kris had ever seen. "And who's this?"

"Kris, this is Ashley. The girl I told you about. She's my friend from school." Kris suddenly remembered their conversation over hot chocolate. He smiled at the young girl, who was gazing at him with her small hands clasped.

Jodie approached them, "Kris, would you like a drink or something?"

Kris smiled, "no, thank you. I'm going to leave in a second."

Reva tugged at his arm, "you can't do that! You just got here!"

"What?" He raised his lips slightly, "you don't want to go to the movies now?"

Reva jumped, clapping her hands, "can Ashley come with us?" Kris suddenly felt the weight of another child on his shoulders.

∽

They had just come back from Jodie's after dropping Ashley home. Kris had spent the morning watching an extremely boring animation film about the discovery of music in a jungle before taking them for junk food and toys. He drove into Adara's driveway and saw her standing by the door, wearing a long, light-grey dress and wrapped in a thick, dark-blue cardigan. He tried not to stare at Adara as he exited the car. Reva jumped out, waving her bag of sweets and toys at her mother. Adara's eyes glowed, clasping her daughter in a tight hug, "inside now. I made some spaghetti."

Reva smiled at him and Kris spoke before she could stop him, "I've got to get going. I'll see you soon." Reva squinted her eyes at him. He felt something fall in him when she let go of her mother with a dimpled frown.

Adara shifted from one leg to another, "there's enough spaghetti, Kris."

Reva clapped, "that's settled!" She ran inside the house and Kris felt his mouth going dry.

He wanted to run back to his car and drive out. He wasn't ready to deal with the rock between them anymore. Adara was standing by the door, holding onto her arm, shifting from one foot to another, waiting for a response from him. He stared at the black stone ring around her neck before turning his head. He exhaled and rubbed his hand through his hair, "I was actually wondering if I could take you to dinner at some point to talk?"

Adara beamed and she nodded slowly while he stepped back to walk away, "it's boiled this time." He halted and gazed at her shrugging, "it's up to you." He glanced at his car and then to her again before his eyes went back to the ring. He rubbed his hand through his hair again before strolling up to her slowly to stand in front of her. He breathed, taking in the scent of the rosemary candles. She lifted her head up towards him and he studied the dimness in her eyes before wrapping his arms around her. He placed his lips on her forehead, feeling Adara's thin arms around his back as her head curled into his chest.

Sunday 9th September 2012

"Why do I get the idea that you come here quite a lot?"

Robyn gave a tender smile before dropping her head. Both Clare and she were sat in Kensington Square Gardens, close to Peter Pan's statue. The statue made her feel magical, enabling her to believe in the power of possibility. She hadn't felt so hopeful in such a long time. She owed Clare so much for the enlightenment she was experiencing. She came here a lot because Peter Pan made her feel young again and reminded her that living can be a beautiful adventure, if she truly desired it to be. She vaguely remembered watching Peter Pan when she was young. She recently watched it again with Clare and was amazed by how much she loved the story. She aimed to read the book next.

The park flooded with a very chilly breeze that made Robyn's arms prickle, even though she was wrapped in a coat. The grass was wet, releasing the scent of nose-tingling damp pollen. She enjoyed it; the smell went straight to her head and reduced that fog in her mind a tad more. She could think slightly more clearly now.

She lifted her head back up and stared at the children playing in front of her. Two girls with long, blonde hair kicking a ball about with what seemed to be their very tall father. Usually this scene would've been morbid for her, today though it brought light to her face. Even if Estella and she had missed out on that, they were on their way hopefully to reforming it.

"Robyn..." Clare helped her to see colours in the deep hole. Even if there was still darkness there, she could also see colours now. Bits of light glittered through and that glitter was because of Clare. It was helping her to climb out of the hole to grasp light. Robyn resisted Clare's suggestion of therapy. She wanted to try and help herself first. Things were building around her, and she knew that would help her to develop herself. She had people around her now. Previously, she had Tim, who helped her to maintain herself, now, she had someone that understood. This was all she needed to turn to the next chapter in her book. Maybe in the future, if she felt like she needed to speak to someone, then she would. She wasn't taking therapy off the list, for now though, she had other support at the top of the list that helped.

"Robyn, I wanted to speak to you."

Robyn giggled at Clare, whose green eyes were filled with worry, "you're not really the nature type Clare, so I figured." Clare pushed her brown beach waves behind her ears. "It's about you and Tim." Clare's eyes shot to her, completely electrocuted. "I'm not dumb Clare. I knew he liked you from the moment he saw you at Kris's gathering. He was gawking at you like he'd never seen a girl in his life." Robyn reached out for Clare's tinkering fingers, "Clare, we were over a very long time ago. I've learnt now that when people enter your life, they enter it for a reason. Tim came into my life to show that I can taste happiness if I really want it. No matter how things are around Tim, he is always happy. I learnt now that he was always happy because he found it in him. He's taught me that if I'm just willing to dig deeper, beyond the surface of myself, I can be happy. It will take time to shed all the layers that have been placed on me over the years, but I can do it." Clare rubbed her arm staring at Robyn, "Tim came into my life so that I could meet you too. You've made me realise that my value lays in me finding value in myself and not through others. I thought I loved Tim and I do, but only as a comfort. He has helped me in ways that he doesn't even realise." Clare took a deep breath and Robyn lowered her head to meet Clare's eyes, "Tim is my best friend which is why I want him to be happy. He's so happy with you."

Robyn's brown eyes flew open when Clare encircled her arms around her neck. She was surprised that she was able to relax into Clare's gesture, so she hugged her back. They released each other and Robyn took a deep breath, whilst turning to look back at the slightly damp grass.

"How are you and Estella doing?"

Robyn bit her bottom lip, "we're getting there, we're just two very different people."

Clare laughed, running her fingers through her waves. "Shall we head back?" Robyn's blonde hair hovered with the wind when she smiled. Clare ducked her head, giggling, "yeah I prefer like, sofas and stuff."

Robyn dropped her head laughing, before she plucked herself up from the bench. A slight wind brushed past her ear and she heard a silky voice, "I'm so proud of you." Clare noticed Robyn freeze when she linked her arm into hers.

Clare's eyebrows pulled together in confusion when Robyn whizzed her eyes around the park. She could hear Clare asking her if she was okay. She nodded, taking Clare's arm in defeat to walk along the grey stubbled path of the park. Robyn tried to keep calm, knowing her mother was somewhere near them.

They walked in silence for a little while, listening to the serenity. The wind brushed past her hair again and her eyes widened. "Robyn, what's wrong?"

"I'm sorry Clare. Just one second." Robyn spun her body around, taking in every point of the park.

"I will always be here for you." Robyn glanced back at Clare and there was Nayla, hovering a few feet behind her. Robyn felt her eyes well up at the vision of her glowing mother. Robyn watched her mother blow her a kiss. She walked towards her, knowing exactly what was happening. "I'm sorry again Robyn. Live curiously. Live joyfully. Live truly." She lingered her hand towards her then dropped it when her mother shook her head. Robyn bit her lips, unable to stop the tears. Clare placed her hand on her shoulder to squeeze it. A chill traced her forehead and Nayla beamed at her. Her breathing halted when she saw her mother wave before stepping back, "I love you darling. Be strong." Robyn sucked in some air, before seeing her mother disappear.

Clare stepped in front of Robyn, searching for an answer to her sudden crying. Robyn dropped her head on her shoulder, and she felt Clare's hand rubbing through her hair. Robyn inhaled before picking her head up and beholding Clare's electric eyes. "Everything is okay."

FRIDAY 14TH SEPTEMBER 2012

The dark streets were just filled with people going in and out of restaurants and pubs. The atmosphere was light and crisp. Adara didn't want to do to anything too formal, so they decided to go to a Mexican restaurant in Paddington. When they left the restaurant to take a walk, they heard people outside pubs mingling.

Most of the talking they had done was generalised and mostly about Reva. He'd wanted to leave the restaurant. The atmosphere was loud and noisy inside in comparison to the outside tranquillity. The cold air helped him clear his mind whilst they walked in silence for a few minutes. He listened to the busy commuters around him trying to figure out what to say to her about the conversation that they both wanted to begin.

"Reva wasn't born here then?" Kris saw her glance at the surroundings from the corner of his eyes.

"No. Erikh managed to get passports somehow from Sai, my brother, and we left the country for Spain. He seemed to think it was best." Adara raised her glimmering eyes wonderingly at the lit path in front of them. She stroked her hair out of her face with her long fingers, "and, looking back at it now, I think it was too. After Erikh died, Sai got in contact with me and told us to come back. I couldn't keep moving around, it wasn't good for Reva."

"How did Erikh..."

"Vidia found him. I wanted us to stick together, but for the sake of Reva, Erikh told me to keep going with her. I think something else must've happened with them whilst Erikh and I were running, because they were caught for something else and thrown in jail after Erikh died. Which is how I knew it was safe to come home."

Kris nodded, taking in the weight of her words. "You were at the hotel when we came back to London."

"Yeah, it was a while after my wife died." Kris rubbed the base of his neck and turned his eyes in another direction, "the house was…" He cleared his throat, "a little overwhelming."

"These days you don't get guys admitting something like that." Kris tilted his head and clicked his tongue. "What about your dad? You haven't said much about him."

Kris placed his hands in his pockets, "I wasn't really that close with my dad. I loved him like a son would, but he only ever wanted me to work with him and that was it."

Adara nodded, "well, he probably loves what you've done. I used to shop at Dauni's all the time and then when I came back from Spain, there were chains everywhere."

Kris moved his head back, "wait." He raised his eyebrows at Adara, "you used to come to the clothing store in Kensington?"

Adara nodded, "you think I would've left my daughter with you so many times if I didn't completely know who you were? At first, I didn't recognise you until I came to pick Reva up from your office. Then I realised who you were. My friend used to stalk you after school and stare at you slouching about the till whilst we raided the clothing department!" Kris rubbed his head, feeling the air around him become warm. "You've changed so much since then. You seem to actually like what you do now and you're so much more confident." Kris bit his bottom lip and tilted his head the other way, not feeling any trace of confidence in him. "I remember when my friend asked you out. Your face went completely bright red before you said no. It'll be interesting to see that expression now." Adara giggled. Kris rubbed his hands over his face, not remembering anything she was talking about. Then he lifted his head up, seeing that they had reached the car.

Kris opened the passenger door and waited behind it for Adara to walk in: instead, she stood at the edge of the door. "Listen," he rubbed the side of his head, "your past belongs to you; your and Reva's future can be with me if you want it to be." Adara stepped towards him. Kris stared at her, dressed in a long black dress and cream-coloured pashmina with matching heels. He saw the spark in her thin black- lined, smoky charcoal eyes until he noticed there was no chain hanging from her neck. With a hint of a smile, he advanced forwards and Adara came closer. He felt something sharp in his chest before he leaned in to kiss her. He heard her giggle and instantly drew back with his eyes open. "What?"

"I thought I was taller." Kris felt the air go warm around him again. He massaged his forehead listening to her laugh, "there's that bright red face."

∼

Kris parked into Adara's driveway, keeping the ignition running: "are you going to come in?" Adara asked. Kris blinked at the house then back at her. "I wanted you to meet my mum." His eyes grew suddenly, feeling his chest become heavy. She squinted slightly at him, "you're nervous!"

Kris rubbed his hand through his hair, "I've never met your mother."

Adara giggled, "which is why I would like you to meet her." She pulled her pashmina over her shoulders, "besides, what about Kelci's parents? Were you this nervous when you met them?"

"I already knew them." Adara's eyebrows raised, "well, Henri, the manager at the store, is Kelci's dad. That's how I met her."

Adara's eyes grew, "Henri! The one with the glasses!" Kris saw her thick lipped smile, "wow!" Adara stared out of the window wonderingly. Kris raised his eyebrows, waiting for her to continue, "you don't think it's crazy how everything just comes back to your Dad's department store? You started dating a girl whose Dad works for the store and now you're sitting in a car with me who, was a constant customer of that same store?"

"When you put it that way, then yeah it's a little crazy…" Kris rubbed his jaw, "but I never dated Kelci." Adara raised her eyebrows, making him shake his head, "story for another day."

Adara stared at him, "everything happens for a reason, Kris." Kris nodded. "Come on. We're going in." He rubbed the base of his neck, "I'm sure you've dealt with harder situations than meeting my mother."

Kris smirked when he switched off the ignition, "well, you're her daughter and you're quite the handful yourself." Adara pierced her large eyes at him and he shrugged his shoulders.

He began running his hand down his shirt when they approached the door. Adara smacked his hand with a giggle the moment the door opened. Reva leapt at Kris immediately as they entered the house. "Did you have a nice evening, Reva?" Adara made her way to the garden whilst Reva dragged Kris into the living room to tell him about a boring princess film her nan had made her watch. Kris laughed, "you didn't like it because she doesn't have your fierce nature."

Kris felt his chest go heavy again upon seeing Adara's tall mother walk in. She reminded him of his mother in law; fiery eyes that didn't resemble her daughter's however with an underlying softness under her angular features and sharp jawline. She placed her hands on her hip, "and I take it this is Kristopher Dauni?"

He suddenly felt like he was back in school, being tested for an exam. He nodded, "yes Mrs Fields, it's nice to meet you, and Kris is fine."

She laughed and waved her hand, "it's Miss Flores but you can call me Arma. Let me get you a drink." Kris blinked, confused by the difference in names. She waved her hand again and tutted, "sit down." Kris instantly placed himself on the sofa and Adara giggled. The air suddenly felt warm again. He glanced at her, admitting to himself that he could listen to her laugh all day.

Friday 21st September 2012

Kris stood in his kitchen with his mug of coffee. He scrolled through his phone for any urgent, unanswered emails. Kris had been spending more time with Adara. Their relationship had become a little clearer. Adara had accepted Reva's school issues and Kris had accepted Adara's past. A past that Kris didn't want her to revisit. He wasn't expecting her to forget and he didn't want her to; he wanted her to begin writing a new future.

Kris finished his coffee before making his way out of the door to meet Lauren. She'd rung this morning, sounding slightly frustrated and asked for his help with architects. He'd been to the building many times and Lauren was struggling to find the right architect for her vision. When Lauren told him about the design she had in mind, he was quite surprised by the theme she had come up with. He assumed she would go for bright colours or cool tones, instead she went for a complete dark palette of dark grey and maroon red. She stated she wanted her place to stand out from the others by setting a corporate tone to her salon that would bring along people with money to spend. Within the design they ensured the salon would be spacious and allow capacity to move around with the reception up front, following a smooth transition to the different areas of the salon.

As he arrived, Kris was still trying to stay awake when they met their first architect at ten in the morning. Lauren didn't seem content with what the man was showing her. Kris could see her losing hope by the time they had reached one o'clock with another architect. "Kris, I've now met six different architects. All their old pathetic brains are the same."

They were sitting opposite her salon in a small café across the street. The smell of fresh bread and strong coffee filled the air and parents were mingling whilst their young toddlers enjoyed their desserts. The young waiter came and placed their coffees down on the table before walking away and attending to another customer. He sipped the coffee, tasting its freshness whilst a young baby screamed in a highchair.

Kris narrowed his eyes at Lauren in confusion. She kept fidgeting with the sleeves of her plain blue top, "well, we still have another two, so breathe." Lauren went through her folder, "and we've only seen three today, where did six come from?"

"Yesterday." She sighed, stuffing the folder into her bright orange bag. She twisted on her seat and rested her head on the window they were sitting against, "I saw three yesterday and one of them was actually pretty okay until he showed me a load of ridiculous digits that made me want to throw my coffee at his stupid face." Lauren tugged at her sleeves, whilst biting on her bottom lip, "they see me and immediately begin treating me like a child!" Kris tilted his head back slightly, "I know it sounds stupid, but that's why I asked you to come today." He raised his eyebrows, watching her rub her head, "I don't know if you've noticed, but even when I'm speaking directly to them they only respond to you and somehow with you there, the prices are a lot better than what I was seeing yesterday." She shook her head, "pathetic." She scratched her head and Kris massaged the base of his neck, not knowing what to say to her. She checked her phone, "I'm going to see my mum today." He nodded.

Kris's phone vibrated and he quickly read the message. He lifted his eyes, taking in Lauren's irritated demeanour. "Adara's asked me to pick up Reva from school. I'll drop you to see your mum and wait for you." She nodded. "Have you thought of a name for the place yet?"

Lauren beamed, "Victoria's. After my dad's mum."

Kris gave her a smile.

She placed her back against the window again, waiting for their next architect to arrive across the road. "Lauren." He rubbed his hand through his hair, "I'm sorry." Lauren picked her head up to meet his eyes. She placed her hair behind her ears and raised her thick eyebrows. Kris rubbed the base of his neck, "I just felt like I should say it. I would hate for someone to treat me like that."

Lauren waved her hands, sweeping away his apology, "you're nothing like all those architects Kris. You respond and give eye contact when someone speaks to you. You don't have anything to apologise for. I've seen you at work." She shrugged her shoulders, "like Gal, you don't treat her the way those architects were behaving." Kris looked across the road at the salon, "by the way, you made Ayva office manager…" She tilted her head, "why not one of the others?"

Kris nodded slightly, "you taught her really well." He shrugged, "and, I trust her."

"You made the right choice," Lauren nodded with a smile. "You'd be happy to know she wasn't one of the ones gossiping."

⁓

Children came flooding out of the gates the moment the bell resonated through the school grounds. Reva came running out with her hands waving and her red school bag hanging from her shoulder. She jumped in front of Kris with her broad, dimpled grin and began telling him about her day at school as they made their way back to the car.

Adara had now started extra tuition for Reva twice a week. Adara and Kris concluded that Reva was having trouble understanding the methods of teaching, thus she found it more difficult to comprehend the content being taught. Adara spoke to one of Reva's teachers about this and about the comments that Reva was dealing with. Kris didn't know if this made any difference, but he knew Reva would say something to him if things escalated and he hoped they didn't.

Reva immediately began begging him to tell her about their afternoon plans. He bit the inside of his mouth, explaining their boring schedules for the day. She just shrugged and then her eyes sparked when they landed on Lauren. Kris started the ignition and immediately the two of them went into a lengthy discussion that he didn't get involved in.

Lauren fidgeted with the sleeves of her top when they neared the café to meet her mother. He reached out and squeezed her hand, making her smile slightly. He parked up and Lauren took a deep breath. She left the car and made her way inside the café. "Why hasn't Lauren seen her mother in so long?"

Kris turned to see Reva, who was removing her seatbelt to move forward in her chair. Kris searched out the window for an explanation, "some things are just not as simple as we'd like them to be." Reva bore her eyes into him. Kris glanced out of the window again before turning back to Reva, "what's your favourite film and what's it about?" Reva began rambling about a film that Kris hadn't heard of. She made small hand gestures, describing the imaginative locations and characters. Kris nodded, "I get it. She eventually finds out who she is and realises she loves the thief. Etc, etc…" Reva pouted and crossed her arms, "the point is, that this princess probably didn't want to be kidnapped and locked away. She would've liked to have known her real parents."

Reva unfolded her arms and then leaned in, "but then she would've never have met…"

Kris touched the tip of his finger on Reva's forehead, "you're clever. She can't control other people's actions, can she?" Reva gently swung her bob side to side, "she can only control what she does, right?" She nodded in a daze, "things are not that simple, but she took advantage of her complicated situation when the thief appeared. She saw an open door and bravely went straight through it."

They went quiet for a while, watching some of the people walking in and out of the shops, "things weren't simple when Dad went and Mum and me had to keep going to different hotels." Kris saw Reva's face transform into a dimpled smile, "but then you turned up."

Kris smiled at her, "your dad was really brave, Reva."

Reva's eyebrows pulled together, "you never met him. How do you know?"

"Because of the way you are." Kris rubbed his hand on Reva's head to mess up her neat bob, "you fearlessly make conversation with nearly every complete stranger in London!"

∼

Lauren and her mother Anne had sat for an hour talking before they made their way to his car. Kris insisted on dropping Anne home before she finally got in and sat in the front with her bag on her lap. She greeted Kris with a bright smile. Anne reminded him of the time when he had first known Lauren; she had the ability to make everyone feel comfortable around her.

On the way to drop off Anne, Lauren guided him through the streets of Kensington, hoping he wouldn't get stuck in traffic on the way back. The roads were soon to hit peak time, so he drove quickly. "Anne, please just call me Kris, Lauren calls me every name under the sun, it wouldn't make sense for you to call me Kristopher." Lauren gasped and saw her mother shoot her beady eyes at her. He tried to maintain control of the steering wheel when Lauren shuffled further into her chair to hit his shoulder. Reva sat laughing in the back seat. Lauren moved back in her seat, pursing her lips at him from the rear-view mirror. "You call me a grumpy, sad, lonely man all the time!"

Reva placed her hand over her mouth laughing, "Kris, isn't that grumpy." Kris raised his eyes at the rear-view mirror with his mouth agape. Reva's dimpled cheeks burnt red when Lauren burst out laughing, "What?"

"I'm not that grumpy? In other words, I'm sad and lonely but only a little bit grumpy."

After twenty minutes, Kris made his way back to his place, "when you get annoyed your eyes go like chocolate coloured marbles, like this." Reva made circles with her fingers and placed them against her eyes, pretending to analyse the car.

Kris turned into his street and then rolled his eyes when Lauren giggled. "You know it's true when a child says it." He wanted to defend himself, however something caught his eye that made his chest spring into a knot. "What's wrong?" He lifted his foot from the gas, pulled the car to the side and removed the keys from the ignition. His eyes remained fixed on the black Jaguar outside his house. He swallowed and exhaled, keeping his thoughts intact whilst his finger stroked the side of his metal key. He recognised that car; it used to belong to his father when he was a teenager.

"Kris?" He smiled weakly into his rear-view mirror.

"Reva, you're going to go back to Lauren's." Reva nodded silently. Lauren's jaw dropped slightly and he directed his eyes straight at her, "you're going for a drive. Eat. Then go back to yours."

Lauren stared at him, "has this got to do with that car outside your driveway that I've never seen before?" Kris separated the car key from his house keys.

∽

Kris's chest felt heavy when he forced his steps past the black car that stirred many teenage memories. He approached his door, ready to place the key in the lock, when it flung open before him. His eyes bolted open when he saw Clare standing in front of him. He stared at her, waiting for her to say something. She stepped out in front of him, bringing a weak smile to her face before moving away. Kris grabbed hold of her arm and he gazed at her before she turned her face with a smile. Kris studied her mute expression. Unlike her sister, Clare was capable of hiding everything she was thinking when she needed to. She rubbed his arm and he let her go. She left the driveway without looking back. Kris swallowed and took in a deep breath before he entered. He laid his keys on the side table, hearing Tim shout to him.

He lifted his head up; everything began spinning around him. A tight knot in his chest pulled in all directions making his breathing run faster than the images in his brain. He watched his hand stroke Kelci's arm before it crawled up and wrapped around the side of Kelci's neck. His mother's voice replayed in his mind, building up a nasty taste in his mouth. He stepped back beside the open door, growling, "before I get to five, you're going to leave my house." Tim stood up with his mouth agape. Kris kept his eyes on Jack, who didn't move from his sofa, "maybe your ex-wife didn't pass on my message for you to stay away from me or anything else that is to do with me." Tim blinked rapidly, however Jack made no attempt to move. Kris knew what he was doing. "One." Tim approached him and Kris took a deep breath, trying to ignore the sensation of Kelci trembling in his arms when Jack glared at her.

Jack still didn't budge and the smirk on his face raised the heat in the atmosphere. Kris breathed deeply again, realising he was sitting in the place where he had passed that drink to his father. He stepped towards the sofa, "two."

"Kris, what the hell is wrong with you!?"

Kris towered over Jack and Tim shuffled in front of him, placing himself in between them. "Three!"

"Kris!" Kris clenched his teeth, knowing this was what Jack was after. Tim pushed him back, "Dad, I think you should leave." Jack still didn't budge, instead he sat staring at Kris.

"Four!" Kris grabbed hold of his hair and brushed his hands over his face.

"Kris, tell me what the issue is!"

Kris faced Jack, hearing his heart thumping louder than his own voice when he spoke, "yeah, go on. Tell him what the issue is." Jack shrugged and the pain in his chest turned into sharp blades stubbing him from the inside. Tim caught him the moment he leapt forward to spring at Jack, making his feet slide backwards on the marble. Jack bounced up from the sofa with no intention of aiming for the door. Kris shrugged Tim off and then straightened himself. He slowly approached Jack with Tim tailing behind him, "or maybe you're too ashamed to speak about how you behaved towards my wife in front of your son."

Jack glared at Kris and he noticed how the skin around his eyes had thickened, "I've got nothing to be ashamed of."

Kris dived to clutch at the little bit of hair on Jack's head. Though Tim bounded towards them, Kris ignored his cousin's shouting. Kris noticed Adara park up in his driveway when he chucked Jack on his doorstep. Jack hastily pulled himself up and Adara stepped around him, disregarding his presence. Tim didn't go after Jack; he instead watched his father reverse out of the driveway in a rush. Kris glanced at Adara walking up the stairs, then confronted Tim, "you can go or stay, it's up to you, just don't mention your father."

Tim advanced on him, "you had no right to treat my father like that. Explain."

Kris rubbed his hands through his hair. "I've got every right!" Tim stepped forward with his teeth gritted, waiting for an explanation, "you should have stuck around to find out why your parents got a divorce."

Blood filled Kris's mouth when Tim's fist met his jaw with full-blown sharpness. He knelt down, holding his face in his hands and closing his eyes to let the intensity of the pain flow. Adara came running down the stairs to stand facing Tim. Her eyes levelled his, "you should leave."

Kris made his way to the sofa, hearing the door slam behind him. "Reva's with Lauren." After a few seconds, Adara sat next to him and handed him a towel wrapped in ice that he placed against his jaw. He hissed, "thanks."

Adara looked at him, studying his face whilst he paced his breathing by concentrating on the marble beneath him, "you didn't hit back."

Kris closed his eyes, "he isn't the one I've got a problem with." Kelci's small, disgusted expression from Jack's large hand crawling up and down her arms entered his thoughts, "he just wanted me to attack him back in front of his son. It's a game to him."

Adara's head moved back, "that was your uncle?"

Saturday 22ⁿᵈ September 2012

Kris heard that ringing voice and he opened his heavy eyelids to have the breath knocked out of him. Every part of her was innocent and natural. No makeup and still a complete doll, with her long locks and eyes you could drown in. He took in the greenery around him, letting the wind in the trees pace his breathing, "I'm so proud of you." Kris wrinkled his eyebrows at her, "you were perfect."

Kris dropped his gaze, "I feel stupid. I don't understand why I didn't just…"

Kelci tilted her head, "what would that have got you?"

"Satisfaction." Kris blinked away from Kelci's emerald eyes. "I made it very clear that I'll call the police if I see him again."

Kelci tilted her head so that her electric eyes shot right into him, "Aunt Louise is too involved."

Kris sat up straight, "so, I just continue letting him get away with it?" She shook her head. "Kelci, he was sitting in our house thinking that everything's okay!"

Kelci stared at him, "Kris, he's bored. He's thrown away everything. He's alone and lonely. He was trying to gain something last night from his son. But you were amazing. You threatened him, but you didn't hit him. You just wanted him gone." Kris rolled his eyes, "he'll get what's coming to him, Kris. This Universe never leaves anything undone."

Kris stared at his wife whilst her large eyes dazed at the sight around them. They listened to the sound of the trees rustling and the water flowing ahead. Kelci fiddled with her fingers and he shifted closer to wrap her hands in his. This was what he'd been searching for ever since she'd died, and he sighed deeply, knowing he wouldn't find this home again. He swallowed, "Kelci, no one can replace you."

"Don't explain yourself Kris." She placed her small hand on his cheek, "I'm so happy for you."

A tear rolled down her cheeks and he instinctively placed his hands on the sides of her face before leaning in to feel the softness of her lips. Something tugged at him. He drew back from Kelci and shook his head. He stared at her before he felt a tug and was instantly pulled backwards. His breathing stopped before he felt the marble floor beneath him. "Crap!" He held onto his arm whilst he positioned himself upright. He rolled his eyes at his mobile vibrating on the sofa behind him before answering, "what!?"

"Bloody hell! Good morning to you too, grumpy!"

Kris let go of his arm to rub his head, "sorry just..." he sighed, "weird dream. And then I fell off my sofa."

"Weird dream." Kris cleared his throat realising she understood. Her tone lightened. "A night on the sofa with miss stroppy."

Kris rolled his eyes, "it wasn't like that." He heard his phone beep; he immediately switched caller, "Tim?"

Kris hung up the call after Tim said he would come around to see him. He had spent the evening telling Adara about his mother, father, Jack and Kelci, although he left the part out about Kelci's ghost. If she could be honest with him, it didn't make sense if he wasn't. He rubbed his jaw and winced. He totally forgot about it. Adara held out a mug of coffee with her eyes wide open and bottom lip quivering slightly. He straightened his back, "what's wrong?"

She traced her finger around the edge of her coffee mug, "I don't want you to feel like I'm being..." she blinked, biting her bottom lip and Kris just continued staring at her, "...pushy."

His eyebrows lifted, "you only handed me a cup coffee Adara, am I missing something?"

Adara rolled her eyes before sitting down on the floor next to him. He turned his body around to face her, "please don't think I'm being pushy. And, I already feel really nasty saying this." Kris wanted to laugh at her blinking expression. He waited a few seconds before she swallowed and spoke down at her feet, "are you planning to remove your wedding ring?" Kris's eyes widened like he'd just been caught cheating. His sight flickered to his left hand holding the coffee mug before he placed it down beside him. "I'm not saying I want you to remove it right now. It's just..." Kris raised his hand, silencing her and feeling a brick drop right through his chest whilst trying to keep his features intact.

Adara retreated from him and he tutted, pulling her back by the arm. He rubbed his head, "I meant that you don't have to continue talking because I understand." He thought about the black stone ring that he waited so long for her to remove. She needed that same commitment and was waiting for him.

She put her head down, "I know she still means so much to you. And it's okay that she always will. I don't want you to get rid of your wedding ring because..." She dropped her head, "I'm sorry."

Kris lifted his head up, exploring her dimmed eyes, "Adara, you don't need to feel guilty for asking me. You've got nothing to be sorry for." She continued looking at her feet, "Tim's coming over. I was wondering if after you wanted to get Reva and we can get some lunch or something." She nodded. He tilted his head down to look at the dim in her eyes. He dragged her closer to him and placed his arm over her. The scent of rosemary overtook his senses when she rested her head on his chest. He winced, trying to place his lips on her forehead. She giggled, before lifting her head and placing her lips against his gently.

∽

A few hours had gone past and Adara went to Lauren's house. She must've decided to stay there a while, because he hadn't heard from her. The doorbell rang and he instantly went to answer it. Tim stood at his doorstep with his hands in his pockets. Kris stepped back for him to come in and he rolled his eyes, watching his cousin walk in slowly, "Tim, you're behaving like you've never been here before." Tim grabbed him and Kris felt the anger in his tight hug before he let go.

Tim followed when he made his way to sit on the sofa. He watched his cousin staring at the wall, until he finally squinted at him, "sorry about your..." Tim pointed at his face.

Kris chuckled, "jaw." Tim dropped his head, taking in a big gulp of air. "You'll get past this."

Tim clenched his jaw, "once he is behind bars." Kris shook his head. "I don't know why you didn't do that in the first place."

"Aunt Louise could possibly get in trouble for withholding evidence of a crime that she knew had happened from the beginning." Tim's eyes widened, "Aunt Louise knew something was happening, but it was only until after he died that she put the pieces together. And by the time I found it out, it'd been too long. If I had gone to the police at the time, then it would be showing that she was helping your father by not confessing earlier. If you go now, then you place not just your mum, but also me in danger."

"This criminal law shit is too complicated," Tim got up from the sofa, "I need a drink." Kris placed his elbows on his knees, gazing at the picture in front of him with Aunt Louise, his mother and Kelci, "how can..." Kris looked at him, "I don't understand how you get on with your life knowing he's still out there."

"Your father isn't a mass murderer. He is a pathetic, jealous coward that killed his brother because he wanted..." Kris exhaled, then rubbed the base of his neck.

"He attacked your mother." Kris's jaw clenched, so he kept his head down, "you said something about Kelci yesterday too." Kris's hands began shaking. Tim approached the sofa to sit down next to him, "what did he do?"

Kris pointed at the ground, "we were standing right here. I don't know if he did it to provoke me, but he threatened her by trying to assault her in front of me during dad's birthday party. The night he died." They went silent for a little while. "Clare was here last night."

"I wanted her to meet dad. She stayed for like, three minutes and then stormed out the door. Does she know?"

Kris shrugged, "like Kelci, Clare never liked him either."

Tim nodded, "he isn't going to get away with this, Kris."

Kris swallowed. "We've already had that conversation, and besides, if needed, I've got him recorded." Tim put his drink down on the table and gaped at him. "After I spoke to your mother, I paid him a visit."

Tim stared at him, "give me a copy of that recording." Kris frowned. "Please." He analysed his cousin's features before he nodded.

They went quiet for a little while again, listening to the clocks in the house whilst continuing to stare at the picture in front of him. "You know, your mum didn't get much from the divorce. She didn't even want it."

Tim turned to him with a stiff look, "after what he put her through, she's owed it."

Kris stared at him, "Tim, one thing I know is that you're

nothing like your father. So, don't let this change you to become like him. Please."

Tim rubbed his head, "but he isn't getting away with what he has put our mothers, you and Kelci through."

Tuesday 9th April 2013

Leaves were now coming to life on branches and flowers bloomed whilst children ran around in their gardens, enjoying the Easter break.

Though Kris knew he hadn't become a different person, everything around him was new and this scared him a little, to the same extent that it excited him. Reva made him feel like he had a purpose in life. She made him want to enjoy life more than usual, because of the strength she gave him. His life was set, and she made him want to take advantage of everything he'd been creating his entire life.

In his memories, Kelci also gave him strength. She reminded him of what he had, what was good and what he could do. This made him continue to move ahead. He missed her all the time; she was still with him in the decisions he made and in the directions that he took.

A few months ago, Kris and Adara made the frightening decision to take their relationship to the next level. He cared for Adara and appreciated having the responsibility of Reva. She brought him life. He enjoyed picking her up from school, taking her to tuition, hearing about how her day went in school and taking her on outings. When Adara and Reva moved in, his home had soul again and he loved the atmosphere. At first, Kris contemplated the idea until the memory of Kelci reminded him to keep going, and he never regretted the decision afterwards.

When Adara unpacked her belongings, she never shifted his parents or wife's possessions; she simply adapted her and Reva's things to his. So now, alongside his family pictures also sat Adara's family pictures. Her dishes sat with his mum's dishes and her books sat with his wife's books. These simple things Kris appreciated. They filtered into each other's space and they welcomed each other's sensitivity. Adara and Reva were now part of his growing family. The three them created time for each other's families and they always made time to spend alone.

The three of them had fallen into a daily routine they that enjoyed. Whenever Adara or Kris were too busy to pick Reva up from school, there was always someone who could: Lauren, Tim, Sai, Arma or sometimes even Aunt Louise. During days off from school, Reva had fallen into an enjoyable habit of visiting Adara or Kris's workplace. She relished being their little helper. Kris and Adara both made plans together for Reva's future and they both wanted to support her in whatever made her happy.

Lauren's salon opened with an immediate rush. Within days, she had customers flooding in and was fully booked for months. Her plans were going the way they'd hoped, and she was bringing in profits exceeding her original expectations; Kris couldn't be happier for her. Her building stood out like no other amongst the other salons in the area and it attracted the customers instantly. She was playing on their curiosity the way she wanted; and she fulfilled their demands, earning outstanding reviews on her website.

Lauren finally agreed to hire Estella and Adara as Kris had asked. Within weeks though, Lauren made Adara team leader due to the quality of work she'd displayed. Adara was also happy to work with Lauren, mostly because she was happy to be closer to home and away from spoilt sixteen-year olds. She was loving her role and she liked the perks that it came with; a better salary, better hours, not having to go to customers' houses, along with free drinks and food for everyone every Friday. Lauren knew how to treat her staff. Adara had to train four other employees and one of them included Estella. Adara admitted that Estella needed quite a bit of training when it came to the practical parts of the work, nevertheless she had excellent customer service skills. She made good relationships with her customers, thus bringing in repeat business and more consistent profits.

A few weeks before Lauren's salon opening, she confessed to not finding the right tech-savvy person. She didn't trust any of the people she knew and though people recommended to her a few digital website designers, she felt she didn't know them well enough. Clare then mentioned that Robyn had quit her job due to being unhappy with the work environment; she was looking for something more creative. After some persuasion on Clare's end, Robyn created a website that complied with the salon's sleek style and spoke to Lauren's quirkiness. "It's as if she read my mind! It was so crazy!" Lauren said to him in amazement, and that was it; Robyn became Victoria's home-based salon marketeer.

Robyn left her old life behind by moving out of her place and renting a new flat with Estella near the salon. Though at times, Kris noticed Robyn struggled to get along with her sister, they were slowly managing to pick up the pieces of their sisterhood. Kris found it nice to see Robyn completely embrace herself. She was talking to everyone a little more than usual and Aunt Louise was happy to get more conversations out of her. Nonetheless, there was something else that Kris and Adara noted; they found it interesting that Reva had created quite a unique relationship with Robyn. It seemed that Robyn found Reva's personality comforting and brought life back to her the way Reva did for Kris. Adara would tell him whenever Reva would go to Victoria's, she would ask to visit Robyn. Reva would come back saying they went to the park, had an ice cream or went to feed the ducks. Adara didn't mind, because it only meant that Reva had more support in her life.

∼

It was two in the afternoon and Tim had asked Kris to come home early. It was his day to pick up Reva, so Kris didn't mind. They stood in the kitchen waiting for Tim to say something. Tim blinked at him with a wide grin as Kris took two bottles of water from the fridge and handed one to him. "What?"

Tim pointed at the bottle. "Looks like your girlfriend is having quite the health effect on you."

Kris rolled his eyes, "how come you're not at work today?"

"I took the day off," Tim placed the bottle on the table and then tucked his hands into his pockets, "I went out with Robyn today." Kris tilted his head and he slowly put his bottle down on the counter, staring at him. Tim rolled his eyes, "no!" He rubbed his head, "before I go on, Robyn and I were friends for a while before we became a couple. And we still are friends. Also, Clare and I have a very candid relationship." Kris picked his bottle up and took a sip of water whilst he leaned against the kitchen counter, "so, Robyn and Clare are now like…" Tim's eyes flicked around the kitchen, "well you know."

Kris grinned, "I think friends would be the right word Tim."

"Anyway," Tim rubbed his head before exhaling, "Robyn was the only person I could think of to go with me and pick out a ring for Clare."

Kris leaned away from the counter and tilted his head, "a ring?"

Tim nodded before placing his hands back in his pocket and taking a deep breath, "I asked Clare's dad a few weeks back. He seemed pretty happy, but I just wanted to make…"

Kris's owl eyes popped open, "as in, you want to propose to Clare?" Tim scratched the side of his head. Kris stared at him, suddenly realising what Tim was thinking. "Tim, if you asked Clare's dad, why the hell do you care what I think?" Tim's eyes opened wider. Kris stepped towards his cousin and squeezed his shoulder.

Tim dropped his head and smiled, "do you want to see the ring?" He quickly pulled out of his coat pocket a little white box that contained a blue sapphire ring that was surrounded by little white diamonds. Kris blinked, analysing the ring closely and then glanced at Tim pointing at it, "well you see, Robyn told me that Clare always wanted someone to give her a ring that was exactly like Princess Diana's ring, because she's obsessed with Princess Diana. We were searching for weeks; and, Robyn eventually stumbled across this and thought it was…"

"Beautiful." Kris lightly hit Tim's back, "I can't see any reason why she won't love it either."

Tim closed the box and placed it on the counter beside him. He placed his hands back in his pockets and shifted from one leg to the other before looking at Kris. "If she says yes, will you be my best man?"

Kris's eyes widened and his lips slowly turned up. He shuffled his hand through his hair, nodding. Tim's shoulders dropped, staring at the ring on the counter; Kris tapped his shoulder. "She'll say yes."

Tim straightened his back, "can we go inside? There's

something else." Before Kris could answer, he watched his cousin walk out of the kitchen. Kris followed Tim, suddenly sensing something cold was sitting in the air. They sat down on the sofa and Kris watched Tim chewing the inside of his mouth, "so, Robyn has kind of inspired Clare to want to do more to help others. I think she feels restricted by her actual role. She told me she wanted to quit her job and asked for me to join her in, like, getting something started. At the time I said no." Kris frowned, waiting for him to continue. Tim took a deep breath, "then just last month," Tim swallowed, "we sat down and talked, she's going to continue with her job and we're going to build something on the side together." Kris nodded, wondering where this conversation was going, "the reason that I said no to her before is because I was working on other stuff." Tim sighed and then cleared his throat before turning to him, "Kris, I had decided to propose to Clare months ago, but chose not to because of what Mum and you told me." Kris breathed deeply, moving back into the sofa, "I haven't been able to move on with anything until I'd done what I wanted to do. And I didn't want to raise the topic with you unless I had something real to say."

Kris brushed his hands over his face and felt a heaviness form in his chest, "Tim, what have you done?" Tim exhaled and looked down at the ground, "Tim." Kris placed his elbows on his knees, staring at him. The ticking clock was making his thoughts move faster and he dropped his head in his hands, pacing his breathing, "you need to say something."

"I'm set and done. It took me some time. Quite a while actually, but I went in and showed him that he could trust me the way his brother trusted him. Slowly, he signed all his companies over to me. It took months. Not that there was much; but still, I took what he had. Then I left him with enough to live off of for the rest of his lonely life..." Kris's heart raced, "I made him listen to the tape recording. He was shocked and tried to deny everything." Kris rubbed his face. He didn't need the recording to remind him of every word Jack shouted in that office. The way he had to remain composed until he gathered all the answers to every question that hung like a hook and line in his mind. He could still hear Kelci's voice shouting over Jack's continuous screaming, after he listened to how he spoke about her and his mother; they were just pawns in his disgusting game of chess. "He's gone, Kris." Kris eyes sprang open and he snapped his head up, "he isn't in the country any more. I forced him to leave and he didn't have much of a choice after I threatened to hand that tape-recording in. I wouldn't have, but he didn't know that. Kris, the difference between you threatening him and me, is that I'm his son. He was ashamed but I didn't care, and I still don't." Kris leapt off the sofa, twisting his neck and trying to control his hands from shaking. His mind was weaving thoughts together that wouldn't leave his lips. "Kris, you, me and most importantly my mother, are never seeing him again."

Kris had not seen his uncle until he saw him in his house those nine months back. During the intervening years he had tried to never acknowledge his uncle's existence; he just attempted to continue with his life. He could never fully do so though, knowing his uncle was close to him and living without the consequences of his actions. Now, Tim was telling him that somehow his father had left the country completely. Kris's breathing scattered, knowing that his body was trying to release a thick chain around his neck that had been holding him back from moving on. He felt a sudden load of heat rush up to his face when Tim span his shoulders around to see the streams of water running down his cheeks.

SATURDAY 27TH APRIL 2013

Tim had requested Kris's restaurant lounge for dinner with everyone tonight. Everyone was going to be there. Everyone that Kris had made his family throughout the years.

He was sitting in his bedroom, remembering his restaurant opening. It'd been so long ago and yet it felt like yesterday. Before the event, his mother had sat him down exactly where he was placed now and told him that she wouldn't be around long to see him be happy, settled and surrounded by the people that loved him. He wondered if at this point, had she truly known that she wasn't well? Is that why she was so direct and yet so vague and serious?

Though at the time he thought he liked her; he didn't completely realise he'd fallen in love with Kelci. He thought he was proposing to keep his mother happy, as always however, his mother knew the truth way before he did. If Kris were to go back in time and tell himself that he had fallen in love, he would think himself stupid and weak. But Kelci wasn't his weakness, she was his strength and was in every step he took.

Kris gradually got off of the bed and made his way to his wardrobe. He took out a dark-blue shirt that Kelci had given him for one of his meetings in Rome. It was Kris's first time venturing out there and he found a connection for a restaurant chain location there. As always, Kelci was the first to support him.

After getting dressed, Kris checked his hair before placing himself directly in front of the box. He took a deep breath and opened it slowly. His chest stirred, acknowledging the contents of the box. Inside was the album that Kelci had given him for their wedding anniversary. He didn't take the album out; doing so might stop him from leaving the house.

Stacked with the album were a few mementos of their relationship that Kelci had collected. A red cabochon stone that Kelci had nicked from his restaurant the first time he took her there before the opening. Stealing things was against Kelci's morals – she never ceased to astonish him. The stone also reminded him of how angry he'd made her that day.

Kris had surprised her with many gestures for their first anniversary. One of these gestures was a holiday in Fiji. So, she kept the boarding passes of their first holiday together. It was her first ever time going on a plane. In the box were also the little cards Lauren had made him write out for Kelci for their first anniversary. She had kept every single one of them. There was also a scarf in the box that made Kris smile. A few months after their marriage, his father had sent him to meet a client in Paris. This was a chance to meet new people, so he didn't hesitate to go. It never even occurred to him to ask his new wife; she was so furious.

He thought a bottle of perfume and a beautiful red silk scarf would help; it didn't work, so he took her on a cottage retreat in the countryside. She had also stolen one of the sheep ornaments that sat on top of the fireplace. During this time, they'd never felt so young. They were completely cut off from the outside world.

Kris found this box a few months after Kelci's passing and the mementos in there were endless. He was stunned to see some of the things she had collected. Some of the pieces in there that he'd even forgotten about were treasures to her that she'd kept. They were now his.

He checked his watch with a heavy sigh. Before having any second thoughts, he placed his right-hand fingers over his left hand. He felt a sharp pain in his chest from removing his wedding band and placed it next to her diamond encrusted engagement ring and wedding ring inside the box. He quickly placed the lid on top and tucked it back in his cupboard before he could even think to take it out again.

He walked out of the room and shut the door behind him. He examined his bare left hand and felt the hallway move around him. He took a long, slow exhale, removing all the unease from his system.

∽

"Actually, I didn't name Reva. Her father did." Adara stood opposite his mother in law, wearing a long, purple dress with her long, wavy hair hanging by her arms. Her wide, grey eyes stood out framed by the thin eye liner whilst Kris glanced at her, then back at Jiya. Though Kris had made it clear he wanted her to close the chapter of her past, he also told her that the more she tried to hide it, the more people would question her. So being candid without completely telling the full story was what he thought best.

They were standing in the lounge of his restaurant. Everyone was nibbling, drinking and talking. An accordion played lightly from the speakers and the sound of chatter sent a ripple through him to ease himself. Reva was also there, sitting and nattering away to Robyn. He would have loved to have known what they were talking about.

Kris thought he would've felt weird introducing his in laws to his girlfriend. There was nothing to feel awkward about though. His in laws; as he should've expected, were warm and welcoming towards Adara and Reva. Kris left the three of them to talk and found Clare standing next to the alcohol. He raised his eyebrows at her, and she hit his arm when he approached her, "I'm actually wondering where on earth Tim has got to."

Kris placed his hand in his pockets and Clare tilted her neck towards her parents, "that must've been interesting."

Kris clicked his tongue, "I should've known actually it wouldn't be that hard." Clare giggled. "I heard you wanted to quit," he said.

Clare dropped her eyes, "Robyn made me want to." He frowned. She placed her long waves back behind her ears, "Kris, don't take this the wrong way, but what you and Robyn experienced is sort of similar. You both just expressed it differently. You avoided everyone, threw yourself in your work and your drinking. You had people beside you Kris, and at some point, I had you." Kris met her eyes before she dropped her head back down, "Robyn had no one. I want to help people more directly and remind them they're worth something." Clare walked away and approached her parents; he glanced at Robyn.

He turned to order drinks before making his way to the other end of the room. Robyn's blonde tresses were hanging around her round face. Her large brown eyes circled with thick eyeliner lifted up at him whilst he placed a glass in front of her. "It's just lemonade now, right? No alcohol?" He sat down seeing Robyn nod. "What's it like working for Lauren?"

Robyn placed her hands around the glass, "she's amazing! Very patient with me." She tilted her head slightly, "though I do think she worries I may get overwhelmed. But I like it, it gives me a direction." Kris smiled at her, noticing her cheeks go red, "sorry, that was a lot of information."

Kris swiftly shook his head, "no it wasn't. It's nice to hear you speak, actually." Her dark red lips raised whilst her eyes concentrated on her drink. "How's things going with Estella?" She blinked, making Kris bop his head up and down, "if you don't mind me asking."

She cleared her throat, "thank you for tracking her down at the restaurant." Kris shook his head, "it's not the romanticised sisterhood. We're two very different personalities, as you may've noticed when she came around your house and wouldn't let go of your hand." Kris chuckled, remembering how he had felt completely confused in the moment.

"Have you ever thought of meeting new people? Sometimes that strengthens the relationships you already have." Robyn's large eyes travelled back to her glass again. "Don't fall in there." Robyn giggled, making Kris lean into the table, "are you going to tell me?"

Robyn squeezed her lips together before lifting her head up, "I met someone at the park a few months ago." Kris moved his head back slightly, finding the scenario completely cliché. "Yeah, I know it's strange. He saw me with Reva a couple of times and approached me when I wasn't with her. He's great and everything but, I don't know." Kris placed his arms on the table trying to read the way she kept squeezing her lips together. "Don't take this weirdly, but at the beginning of my relationship with Tim, everything was just organic. We didn't have to try." Kris felt something drop inside of him. He remembered how things felt natural with Kelci when they were together. "All couples have their own dynamic, but…"

"I get it." She blinked at him and he leaned into the table, "look, you were with Tim for a really long time, so now everything else is completely foreign." He searched the room for the right words, "Robyn, nothing's cemented. If things don't work out, there'll be someone else in the future. Be you and if it doesn't work out, either way you're stuck with everyone here whilst the right person comes along." Robyn smiled. "you're not alone, Robyn." She gazed at him with her brown eyes wide open. Kris then jumped, feeling a light hand on his shoulder.

Estella dropped herself beside Robyn, clutching at her stomach and pointing at Tim who was rubbing his head, "this twit here decided to lose the ring!"

Kris burst out laughing. Tim rolled his eyes, "why would I *decide* to lose the ring?"

Robyn raised her hands, interrupting the run of their argument, "have you at least found the ring?"

Tim picked up Kris's glass and chugged all the contents down before slamming it down on the table, "it was in Kris's kitchen cabinet."

Kris's eyes grew, "it was missing for that long and you didn't notice!"

Estella clapped her hands, "exactly! Thank you!"

Tim stood up, straightening himself while shooting his eyes at

Estella. Robyn raised her arms between the two of them, "okay! You found the ring! Now what!?"

Tim blinked at Robyn and then at the box in his hands. Kris smiled and he stood up to gather everyone around the long table in the middle of the room. He didn't realise Lauren had come too. She placed herself next to Aunt Louise, who blinked at her bright floral dress, which had small yellow baubles of fur scattered on it. He sighed whilst she grinned at him from across the table. He returned the smile and saw Reva settle into the chair next to her before Adara placed herself next to him.

Tim stood up and the chatter stopped, making the sound of music resonating from the speakers more prominent in the atmosphere. "Thanks everyone for coming by the way." He took a deep breath, "I don't really do talking in front of people. So, I'm just going to talk and see what happens." He scratched his head, "I don't really have any regrets, because everything that happened has brought all of you here at the table today. One of my best friends, who helped me mature into a better man today than when she met me." Tim pointed at Robyn and she beamed at him. "I was really worried about coming back and she knew that. She also knew that I was nervous about meeting a frighteningly intimidating version of the Kris that used to play tricks on me when we were children – but who luckily just turned out to be a little more boyish than his childhood self," Kris rolled his eyes, "but I'd like to think I've also become a better person since coming back and I've got Clare to thank for that." Clare's green eyes sparked wide open, gaping at Tim. He made his way around the table to her, "someone would normally have lots of wonderful things to say," Tim went down on one knee in front of her and she shot up from her chair, flapping her hands up and down. Estella burst out giggling and quickly bit her lip to stop herself. Aunt Louise and Lauren covered their mouths with their hands. "…But all I can say is that if you take me to be your husband then I promise to keep being better every day to support you in becoming as happy as can be." Clare covered her mouth as she stared at Tim whilst tears streamed down her cheeks.

Kris gazed at Tim, whilst he chewed the inside of his mouth waiting for an answer from Clare.

"I think this is when you say something, Clare." Estella noted from the table, "a man tends to get a little worried when the girl goes silent!" After a few seconds, Clare went down on her knees with streaks of tears running down her blushing cheeks to hug him.

Lauren halted everyone before they lifted themselves off their chairs, "can he put the ring on her finger first?" Reva jumped from the table to stand behind Clare for a better look at the ring. Clare squeaked, with her green eyes glimmering. She waved her hand lightly in front of Reva and she showed her dimples with a wide smile before wrapping her arms around Clare.

Everyone began raising themselves from their seats to greet the newly engaged couple. "I'm so proud of you my baby girl," Henri said, holding onto her face. Jiya gripped her into a hug. Kris approached them and Clare let go of her mother to envelop him in a hug. Kris kissed her forehead. His sister in law was no longer that younger sister getting random haircuts and trying to find her way; she had now discovered her purpose and grounding in life. She wanted to help people in her career and was ready to get married. "You've come such a long way," he said. Clare nodded. "Kelci would be so happy for you."

Clare chuckled, "she would be jumping like a kangaroo right about now." Kris laughed. Aunt Louise squeezed his shoulder from behind and went to embrace Clare. He quickly walked away, not wanting to get involved in their soon-to-be wedding conversation.

As he walked back to his chair his left arm was tugged back. He turned to see Adara staring at his left hand with her plump grin that reached both her diamond studded ears. She brought herself closer to him, "I know it wasn't easy for you."

Kris looked around the room, seeing everyone lost in their conversations rather than noticing the dinner that was being laid on the table. He saw Reva sitting and nattering away with Robyn, "let's go for a walk."

∽

They'd been strolling for a while now. The weather wasn't too cold that night and Kris revelled in it. The roads were hushed and there weren't many people out on the streets. The pavements were lit with streetlamps, making Kensington look the most picturesque it had ever appeared to him. He glanced ahead in front of him, knowing that the enlightenment in him would dim every now and then, but at least it was still there. That feeling was more than he would've ever expected in his life.

They hadn't said much to each other when Kris held onto Adara's hand in his pocket. "What are you thinking?" Adara's eyes scanned him and she halted to gaze wonderingly at him.

Kris exhaled after breathing in the chilly air, mixed with the scent of rosemary. "I want to adopt Reva."

Adara's black-lined grey eyes fluttered in stunned awe. She bit her lips; he searched her features, trying to understand her thoughts. She placed her hands on his cheeks before she touched his lips with hers lightly, "Reva is just as much your child as she is mine. If it makes you happy to get that written on paper, then by all means, please go ahead and do so."

Kris smiled admiring the brighter colours of his future.

ABOUT THE AUTHOR

Vaneeta Kaur was born in 1991 and is based in London. She is a creative writer and emotional wellness advocate. She is also the author of Broken Branches; the first novel in the Silver Lining series, as well as a soon to be published, stand-alone novel. She is also penning another stand-alone, soon to be published book. She hopes that her novels will provide comfort the way stories have for her.

Her experiences with depression and anxiety have led her on an emotional wellness journey and into a phase of self-exploration. Through her words she wishes to help people to listen to their intuition, hone their perception and bring their imaginations to reality to guide them in understanding how they can create their own peace. Vaneeta does talks and interviews to share her experiences of mental and emotional health as well as her writing journey.

You can follow her through:
vaneetakaur.com
@missvaneetakaur
linktr.ee/vaneetakaur